STAR WARS

REBEL STARFIGHTERS

Owners' Workshop Manual

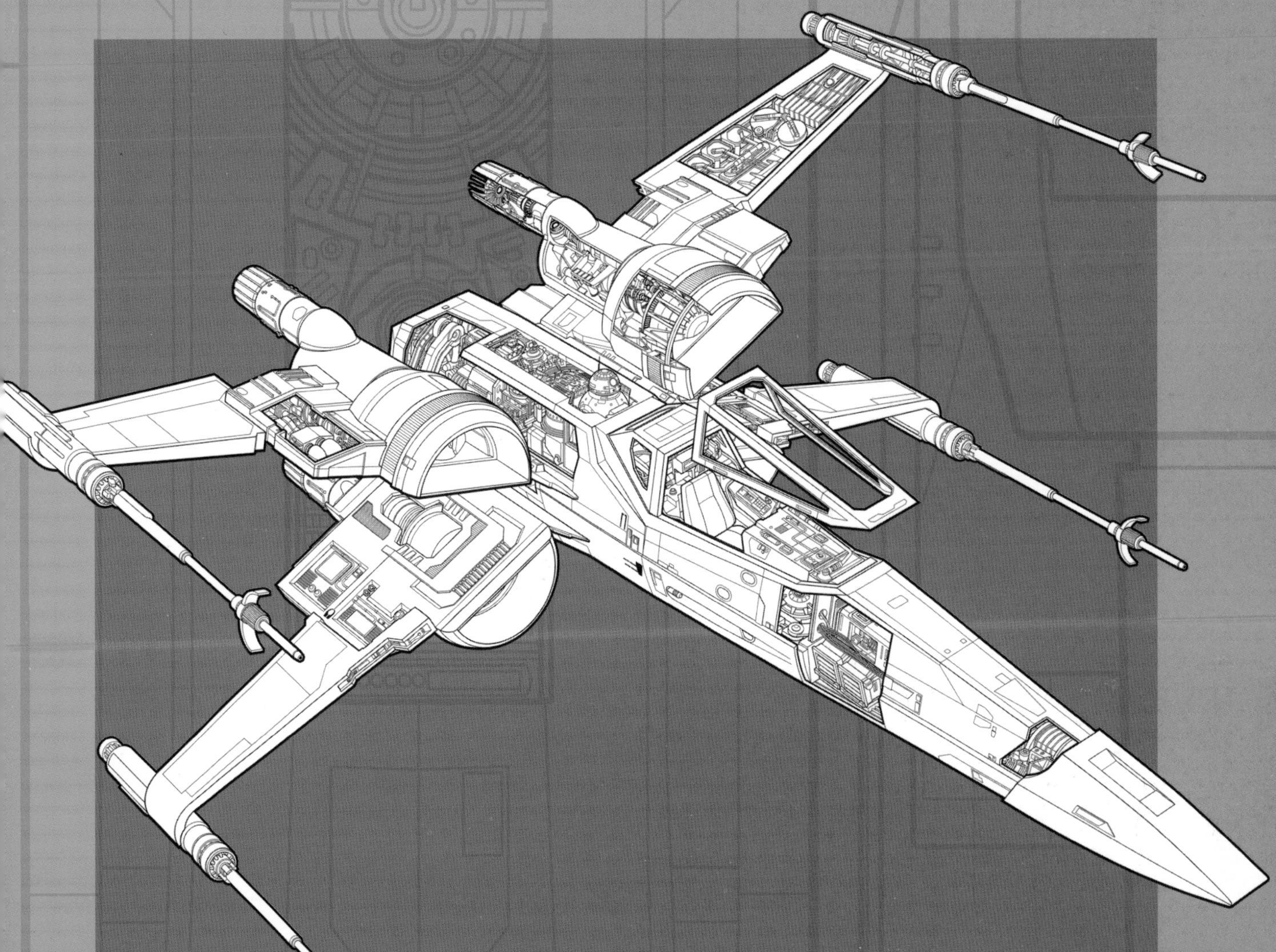

Alliance and Resistance Models

Ryder Windham, Chris Reiff and **Chris Trevas**

CONTENTS

INTRODUCTION

Classified Communique
To: Mon Mothma

From: Leia Organa
Subject: Starfighter assets

I read General Dodonna's report from our field commanders. And I agree, the Alliance's strongest starfighter assets are the X-wing, A-wing, U-wing, and prototype B-wing. From reports, I understand that the B-wing still presents technical challenges, but if the manufacturer delivers a single-pilot blockade buster, we should take it.

You're aware that I recently helped liberate three Hammerhead corvettes and all the supplies they carried from an Imperial spaceport on Lothal. I have information that may allow me to be similarly helpful to our cause.

I believe you are familiar with Captain Raymus Antilles, who has long served my father's command staff. After Antilles learned that the Imperial Security Bureau arrested a group of Incom Corporation engineers and scientists who are sympathetic to the Rebellion, and once he determined that he wasn't walking into an Imperial trap, he managed to intercept an Imperial convoy before it could deliver the Incom staffers to the spice mines of Kessel. He liberated the prisoners, and they were quick to disclose data about X-wings, including the location of protoypes and a potential manufacturer, a remote facility run by outlaw technicians. Using my connections in the Senate, I'm confident I can acquire and divert materials that we can use to build new X-wings. All the details are on the attached datatape.

I realize that stealing used X-wings is more expedient than constructing new ones. However, we can't steal enough starfighters to take on the entire Imperial Navy. If we're to build a strong fleet for the Alliance, we should start some actual building as soon as possible.

Stealing is for the desperate. Building is for the hopeful. And as desperate as we are, we must also have hope.

◀ The Rebel Fleet relied on modified Incom Corporation T-65B X-wing starfighters to serve as escorts for capital ships and medical frigates as well as for combat missions against Imperial ships and installations.

BTL-A4 Y-WING STARFIGHTER

"Some of you may be skeptical about these Y-wings because of their age and condition. And I admit, the designers at Koensayr would probably cringe if they saw how many parts these fighters have lost over the years. But before you call Y-wings 'old junk heaps,' here's three facts.

"First, we need every starfighter we can get. Including fighters with proven combat records. The Y-wing helped the Republic Navy win the Clone Wars. Don't believe me? Think about it. The Republic commissioned the Y-wing for clone pilots to take on the Confederacy's droid starfighters, and last I checked, the droids didn't win. Politics and historical outcomes aside, the fact remains that the Y-wing had more victories than losses in the Clone Wars, and they've still got a lot of fight in them.

"Second, the Y-wing is durable. If they weren't built to last, they never would have made it this far. They may lack their original armor plating, but they can still take a pounding, and they can dish it out too. Each one is equipped with more firepower than any standard Imperial TIE fighter, and unlike TIE fighters, Y-wings have energy shields.

"The third fact is that the Y-wing will help us defeat the Empire. If I didn't believe that, I wouldn't be in this squadron. Our allies took a lot of risks to obtain these fighters, and our mechanics and technicians have made each one faster and more lethal than the Koensayr manufacturers ever intended. As pilots of Gold Squadron, we shall use our Y-wings to inflict maximum damage on the Empire every chance we get. Understood?"

"All right, then. Let's fly."

—Captain Jon "Dutch" Vander, leader of Gold Squadron, addressing pilots at the Alliance to Restore the Republic base on Dantooine.

◀ Resembling skeletal versions of their armor-plated ancestors from the Clone Wars, decommissioned and extensively modified BTL series Y-wings found new life as starfighters for the Rebel Alliance during the Galactic Civil War.

BTL-B Y-WING STARFIGHTER

During the early stages of the Clone Wars, the Republic Navy commissioned Koensayr Manufacturing to develop a combination starfighter and long-range bomber that could deliver more destructive power than the typical Torrent V-19 interceptor or the then-current Jedi starfighters. Koensayr responded with the BTL-B Y-wing, a hyperdrive-equipped fighter-bomber with a wedge-shaped cockpit module that carried a pilot in a forward-facing seat, and a tailgunner in a rotating bubble turret. The cockpit module connected to a reinforced central spar; at the spar's aft, a cross wing carried two large Koensayr ion jet engines. Four strong pylons extended behind each engine to support a long engine nacelle. Because the Y-wing tended to run hot, a complex cooling system extended throughout the ship.

The success of the new fighter-bomber prompted the Republic Navy to commission Koensayr to produce the BTL-B in large numbers, and to also build variant Y-wings for what became known as the BTL series. The series included the BTL-S3 Y-wing, a fighter-bomber with a cockpit that carried a pilot and gunner seated back-to-back in the cockpit, and the BTL-A4 Y-wing, which held a single seat for a pilot. Except for the cockpit variations, all ships in the BTL series were similar in design.

After the Clone Wars and the foundation of the Empire, burgeoning rebel cells began seeking out starfighters to use in their war against the Empire. The Y-wing soon became the workhorse of the Rebel Alliance starfighter arsenal.

▲ Koensayr Manufacturing built the BTL-B Y-wing primarily for identical clone trooper pilots and gunners, but mechanics could adjust the fighter's seats and controls to accommodate other operators, including Jedi, of different heights.

◀ The Republic Navy used Y-wing bombers at the Battle of Malastare, where a clone trooper pilot deployed an experimental weapon to defeat an army of Separatists droids.

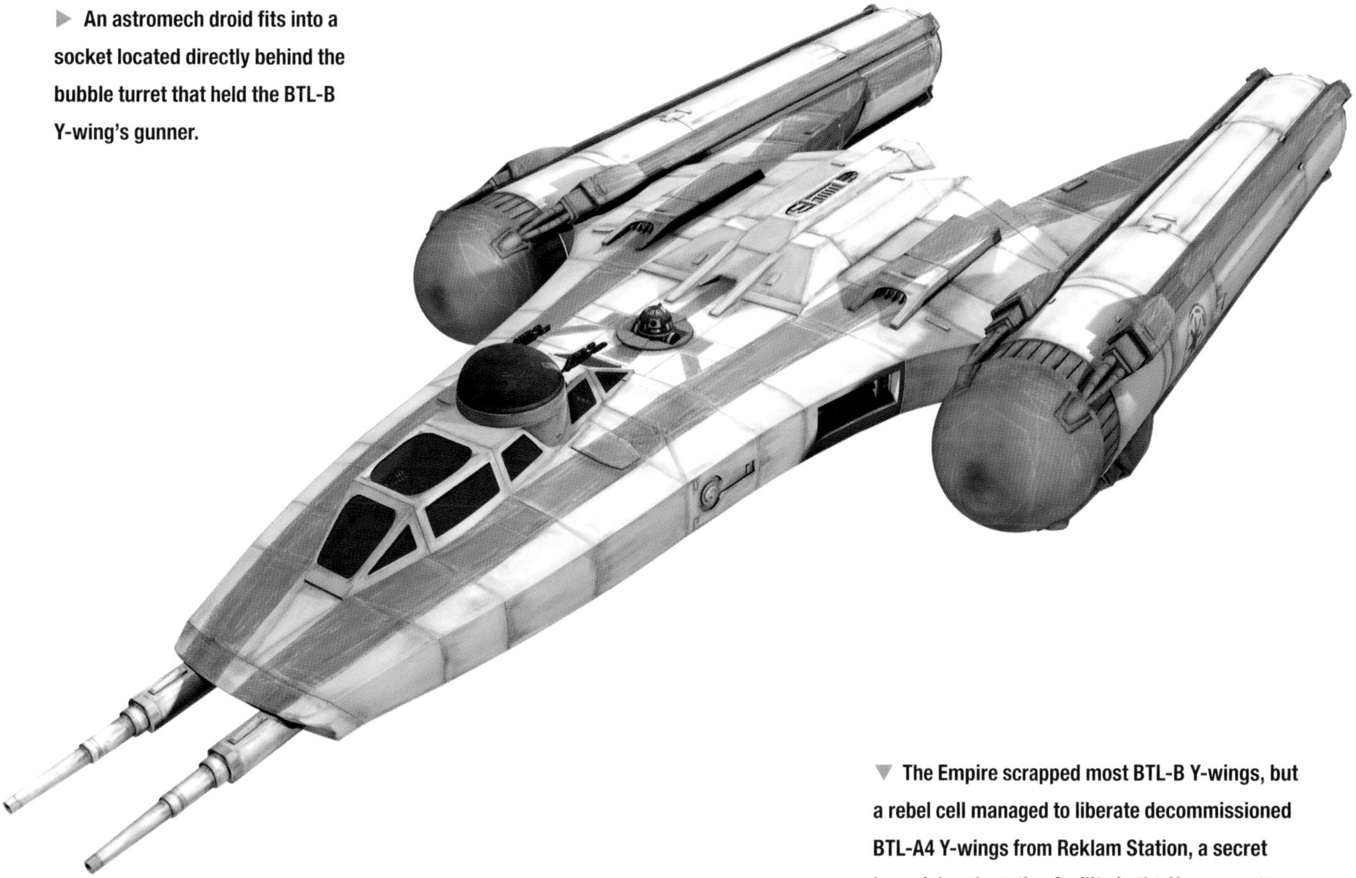

▶ An astromech droid fits into a socket located directly behind the bubble turret that held the BTL-B Y-wing's gunner.

▼ The Empire scrapped most BTL-B Y-wings, but a rebel cell managed to liberate decommissioned BTL-A4 Y-wings from Reklam Station, a secret Imperial reclamation facility in the Yarma system.

BTL-A4 Y-WING STARFIGHTER

Determined to add as many BTL-series Y-wings as possible to their fleet, the Rebel Alliance dispatched search parties to buy or commandeer Y-wings from military surplus dealers and scrapyards. The most commonly available BTL model was the BTL-A4. After rebel technicians and mechanics began making necessary upgrades, modifications, and repairs, they realized that the Y-wing's cooling system would require extensive maintenance and a tune up after every flight. Soon, the flight crews became aggravated by the need to remove Y-wing hull panels in order to access machinery and run diagnostics for each maintenance check.

To more efficiently access various components, the crews decided to remove most of the Y-wing's armor while adding energy-shield power to help defend the ship from enemy fire. Mechanics used the surplus Y-wing armor to refit other Alliance ships, notably the Incom T-47 airspeeder, which they modified for combat and cold-climate atmospheres. Crews determined that the Y-wing's standard fuel recycling system was extremely efficient for long-range missions, and kept the system in place on BTL-S3 models used for courier service. However, crews also realized that the fuel recycling system's heavy weight could actually inhibit overall performance, especially during quick hit-and-run missions, so they removed the system from all Y-wing bombers.

Koensayr equipped all Y-wings with an astromech droid socket. The droid connected directly to the fighter's central circuit matrix and managed all flight, engine, and power systems. The droid also stored necessary data for the Y-wing to make hyperspace jumps.

▼ **Throughout the Galactic Civil War, the single-seat BTL-A4 Y-wing was the most easily available starfighter to the Rebel Alliance.**

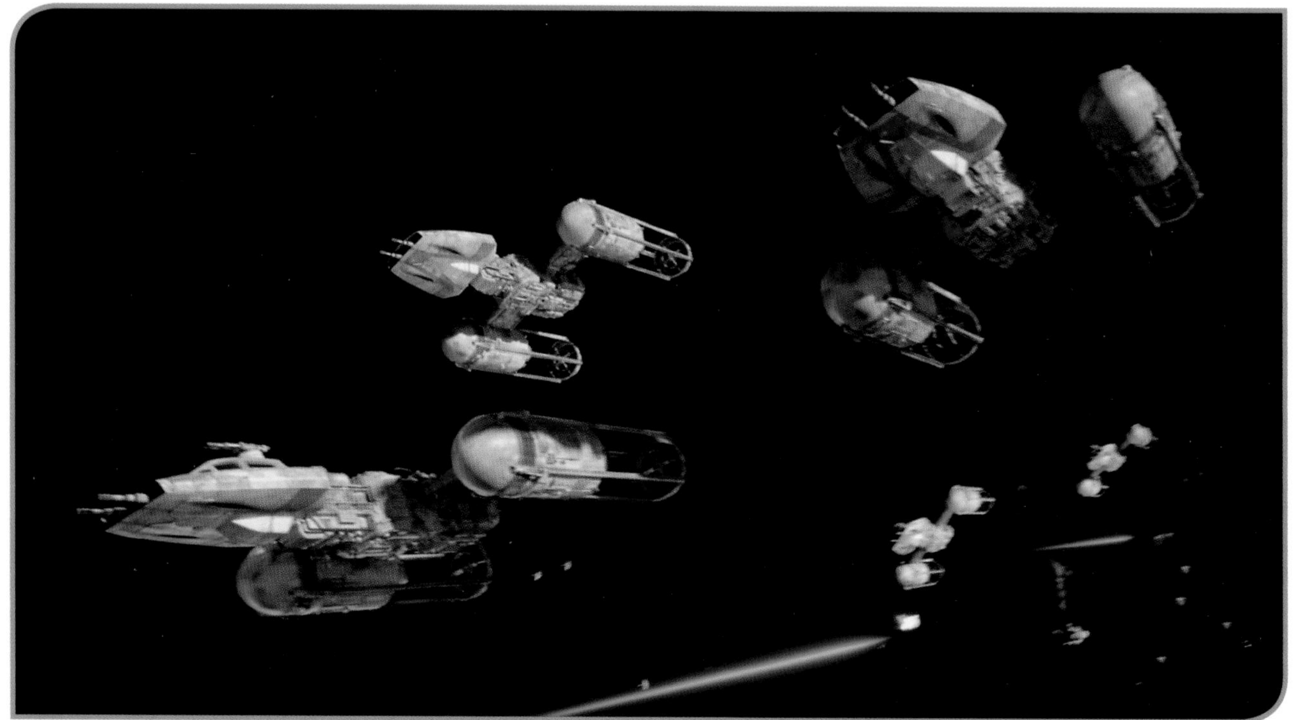

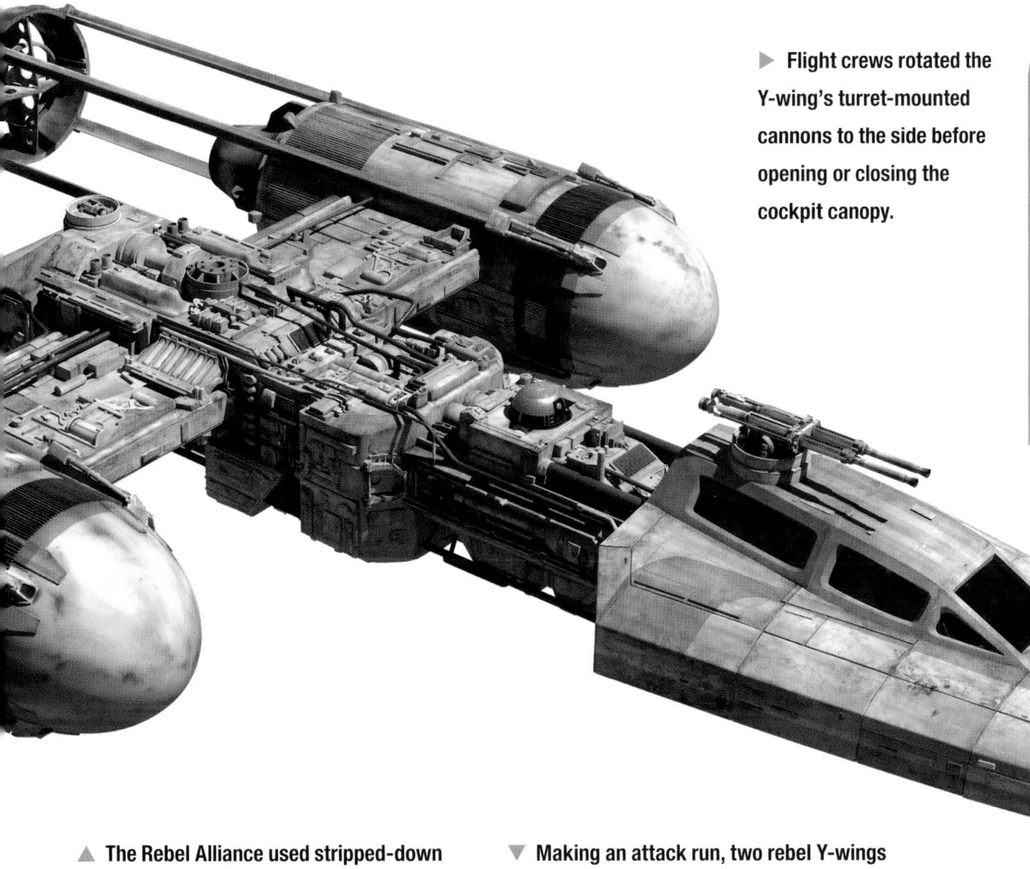

▶ Flight crews rotated the Y-wing's turret-mounted cannons to the side before opening or closing the cockpit canopy.

▲ The Rebel Alliance used stripped-down BTL-A4s for escort duty, reconnaissance, light bombing runs, and surgical strikes.

▼ Making an attack run, two rebel Y-wings speed through a long trench during the mission to destroy the Imperial Death Star battle station.

SPECIFICATIONS BTL-A4 Y-WING STARFIGHTER

MANUFACTURER: Koensayr Manufacturing
AFFILIATION: Alliance to Restore the Republic, New Republic
MODEL: BTL-A4 Y-wing
CLASS: Assault starfighter/bomber
ORIGINAL LENGTH: 23.04 m (75ft 7 in)
Rebel-modified length: 16.24 m (53 ft 3 in)
WIDTH: 8.54 m (28 ft)
HEIGHT: 2.44 m (8 ft)
MAXIMUM ACCELERATION: 2,700 G
MEGALIGHT PER HOUR: 70 MGLT
MAXIMUM SPEED (ATMOSPHERE): 1,000 kph (621 mph)
ENGINE: Koensayr R200 ion jet engine (2)
HYPERDRIVE: Class 1 Koensayr R300-H
SHIELDING: Chempat deflector shield generator
NAVIGATION SYSTEM: Astromech droid
TARGETING SYSTEMS: Fabritech ANc 2.7 tracking computer
ARMAMENT: Taim & Bak IX4 laser cannons (2) or Taim & Bak KX5 laser cannons (2); ArMek SW-4 ion cannons (2) or SW-5 ion cannons (2); Arakyd Flex Tube proton torpedo launchers (2); proton bombs and torpedoes
ESCAPE CRAFT: Ejector seat
CREW: Pilot (1); astromech droid (1)
LIFE SUPPORT: Equipped
CONSUMABLES: 1 week
COST: 135,000 credits new; 65,000 used

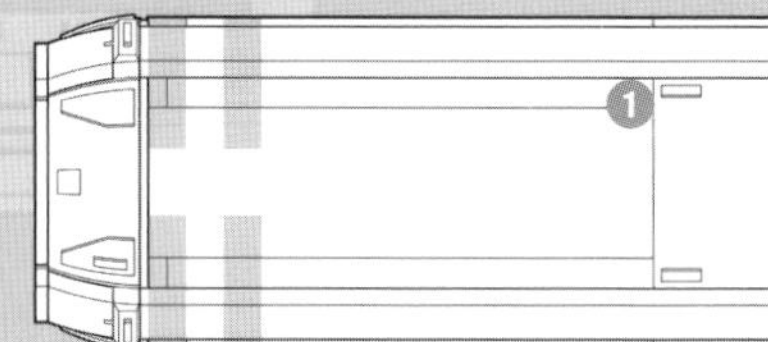

Rebel mechanics removed the Y-wing's original transparisteel bubble turret and installed automated twin ion cannons.

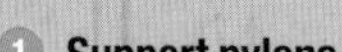

1. Support pylons
2. Heavy ion jet turbines
3. Long-range targeting sensor array
4. Heat vents
5. Astromech droid socket
6. Ship-to-ship photonics comm system
7. Neck repulsorlift
8. Ion cannon
9. Torpedo launch tube
10. Laser tip
11. Composite sensor dome
12. Main power cell
13. Wing repulsorlift
14. Cooling intakes
15. Rear sensor
16. Deflector shield generator
17. Hyperdrive tachyon exhaust
18. Hyperdrive sequencer
19. Deflector shield projectors
20. Main coolant pump
21. Titanium-reinforced Alusteel hull
22. Squadron markings
23. Cockpit pod ejectors
24. Emergency floatation system
25. Life support equipment
26. Transparisteel bubble turret
27. Cockpit canopy

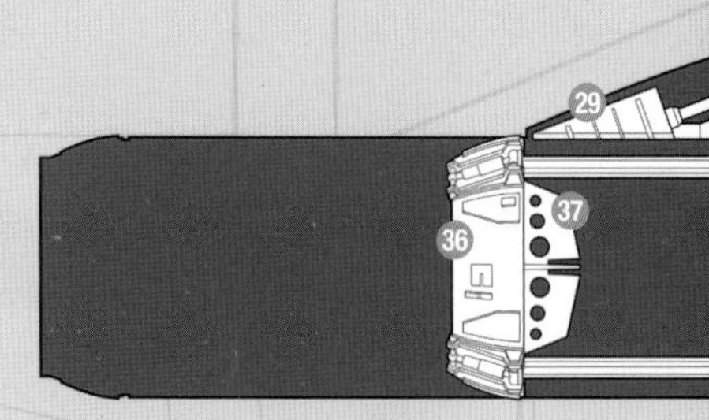

REBEL MODIFICATIONS

- 28 Reinforced tail
- 29 Fuel reclamation
- 30 Electromagnetic gyro filter
- 31 Backup batteries
- 32 Secondary life support
- 33 Fresh water tanks
- 34 Proton torpedo launch racks
- 35 Power coupling
- 36 Vectral ring
- 37 Thrust vectrals
- 38 Exhaust nozzle
- 39 Turbo modifications

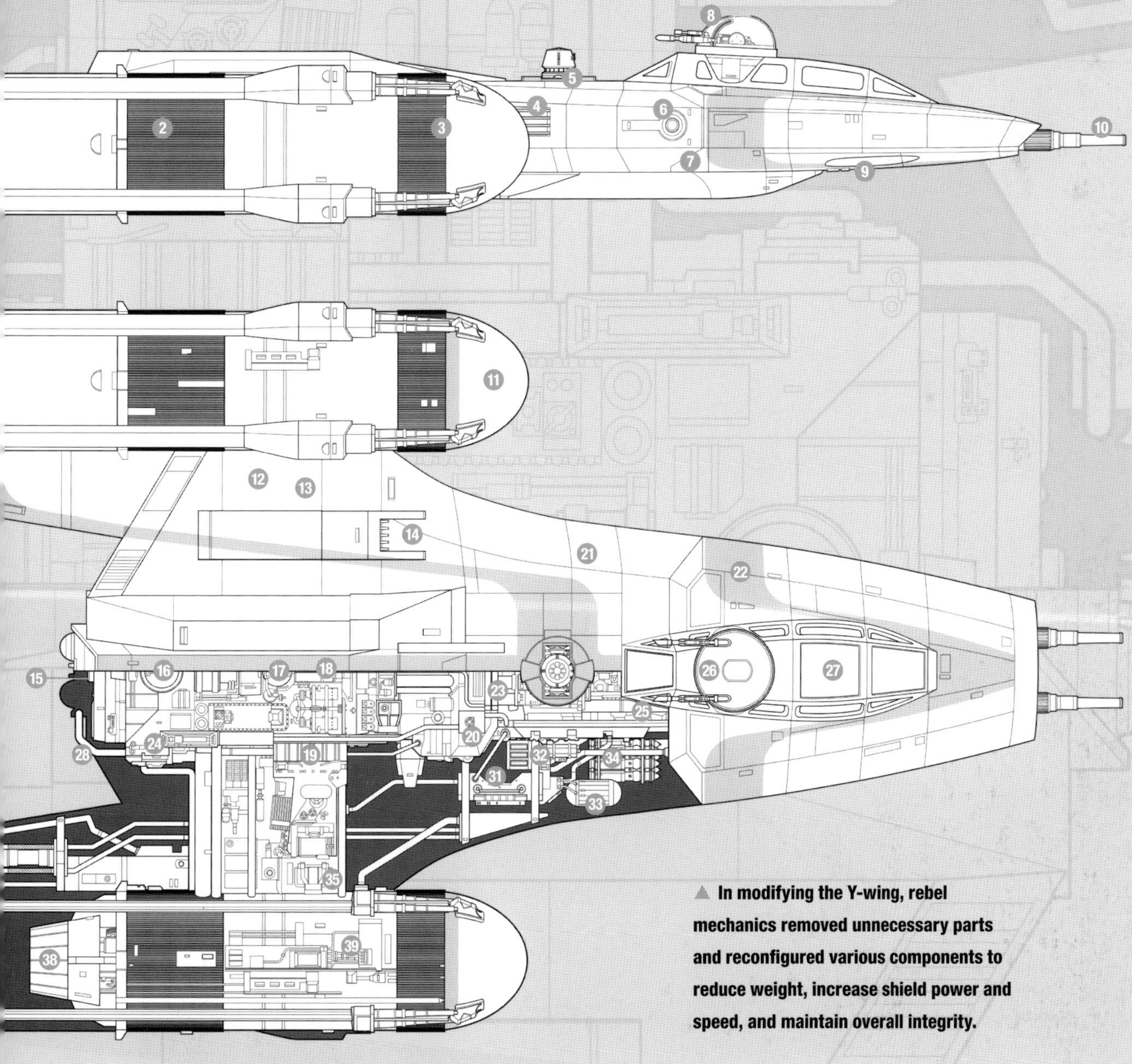

▲ In modifying the Y-wing, rebel mechanics removed unnecessary parts and reconfigured various components to reduce weight, increase shield power and speed, and maintain overall integrity.

VIEWS

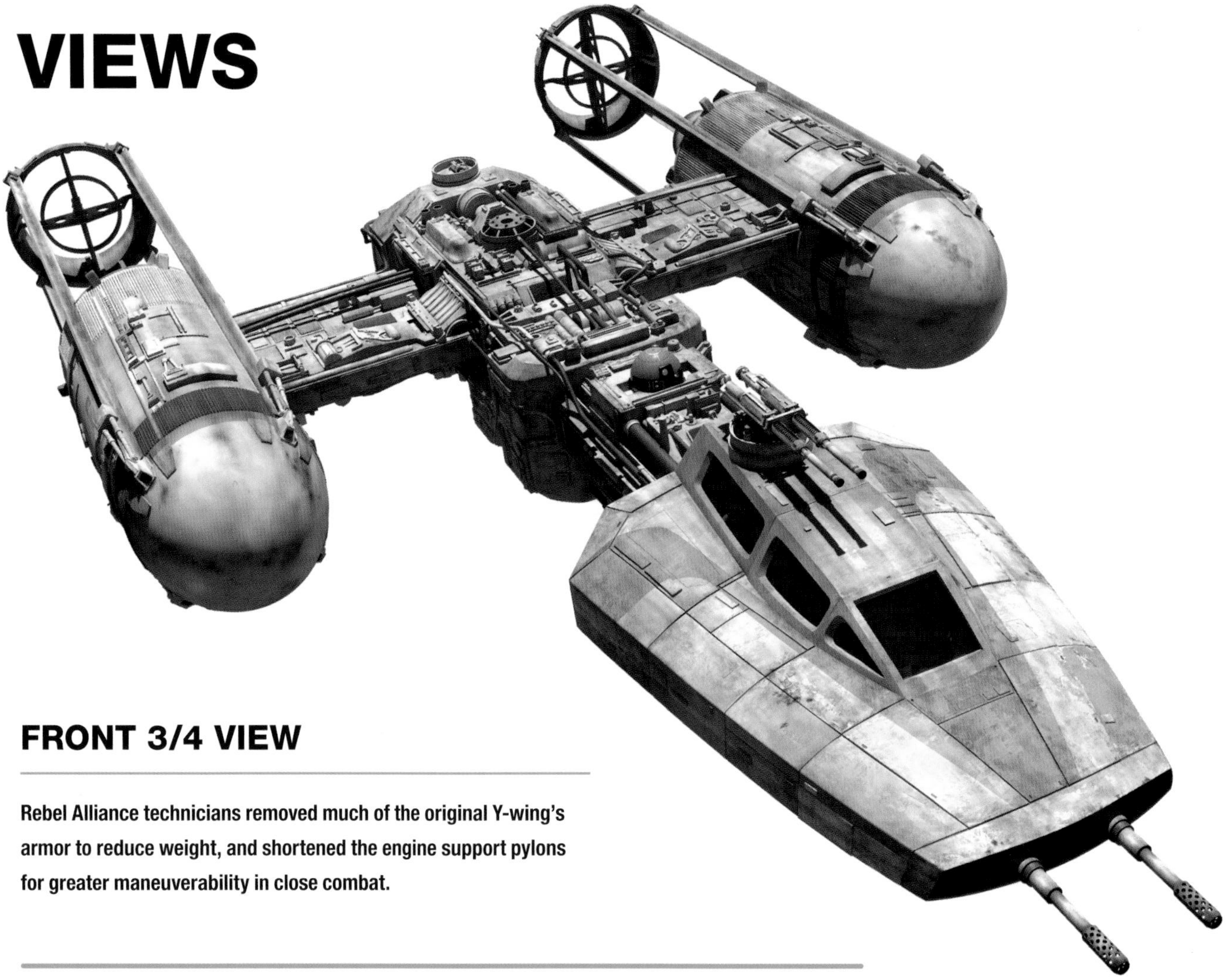

FRONT 3/4 VIEW

Rebel Alliance technicians removed much of the original Y-wing's armor to reduce weight, and shortened the engine support pylons for greater maneuverability in close combat.

PORT VIEW

An astromech droid, positioned in a socket behind the Y-wing's cockpit, managed navigational duties and emergency repairs.

DORSAL AND VENTRAL VIEWS

Lacking the original BTL starfighter's armor plating, the rebel-modified Y-wing appeared relatively spindly, but the modifications did not compromise the ship's overall integrity.

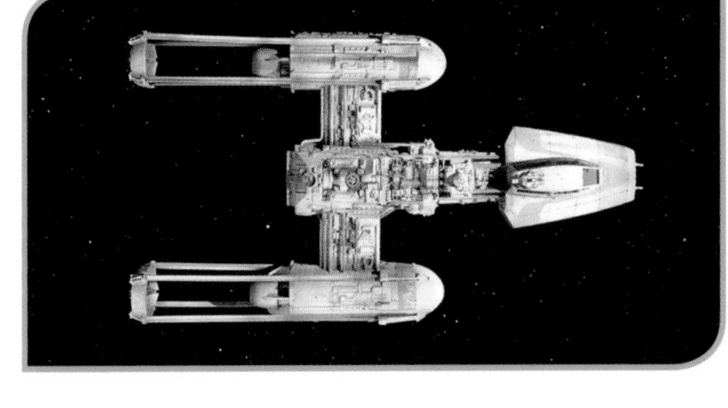

FORWARD AND AFT VIEWS

Two thruster control jets in the aft-face off the Y-wing's central spar gave the fighter great maneuverability. Disk-ventrals, set in the end of the engine nacelles to redirect thrust, provided additional agility.

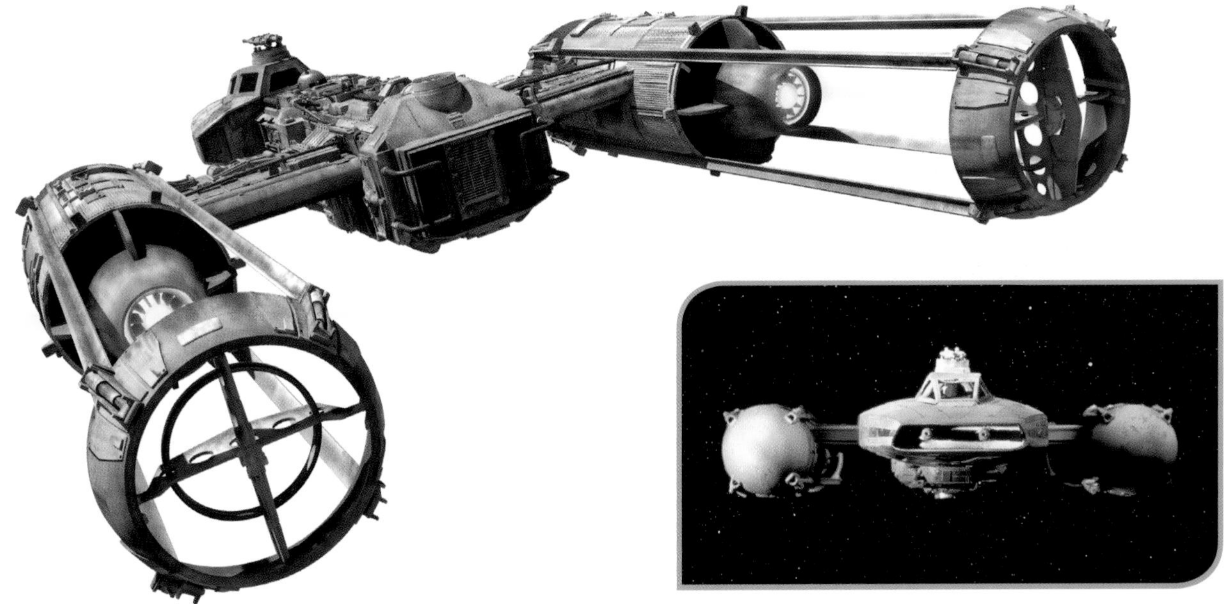

BTL-A4 Y-WING COCKPIT AND FLIGHT CONTROLS

The original Koensayr BTL-B Y-wing bomber cockpit held a forward-facing seat for a pilot and an elevated aft seat for a tailgunner inside a rotatable transparisteel bubble turret. Konesayr subsequently produced the BTL-S3 Y-wing, which held tandem back-to-back seats: a forward-facing seat for a pilot, and a rear-facing gunnery station. A BTL-S3 variant held tandem forward-facing seats, with the rear seat designated for a gunner or passenger. Yet another variant, the BTL-A4, was essentially a single-seat version of the S3, but with the gunner station removed and the ion cannon locked down. All Y-wing cockpits featured transparisteel canopies, pressurized life-support systems, and Guidenhauser ejector seats. Technicians modified some Y-wings to have detachable cockpits that served as repulser-powered escape vehicles.

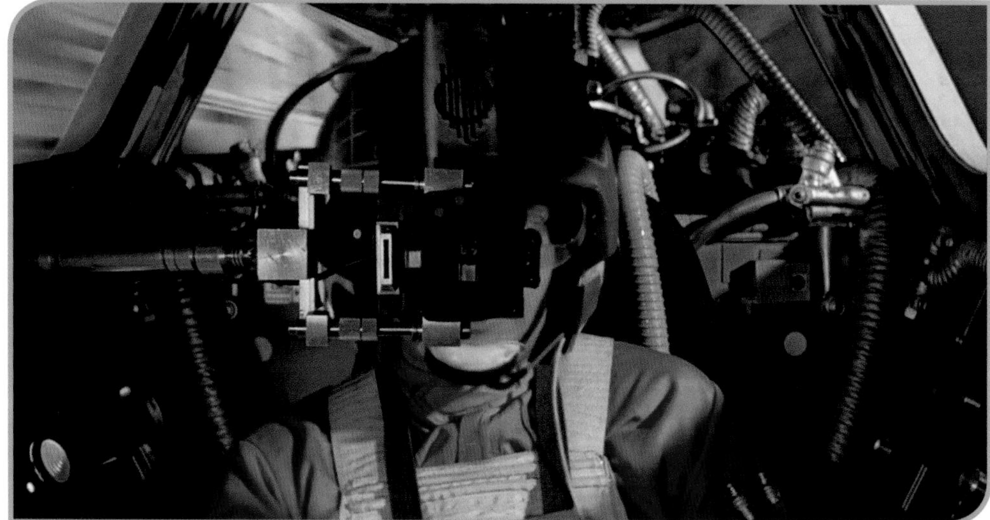

◀ **A targeting computer screen mask extended from a console located at the fore-starboard side of the Y-wing cockpit.**

▼ **Through the computer screen mask, pilots viewed the electronic crosshairs of the Y-wing targeting computer's gunsights.**

BTL-A4 Y-WING CONTROLS

1. Display monitor
2. Warning lights
3. Accelerometer
4. Velocity indicator
5. Attitude indicator
6. Deflector shields
7. Altimeter
8. Sensor scope
9. Computer indicator
10. Autopilot/astromech monitor
11. Landing controls
12. Flight suit hose input
13. Air scrubbers

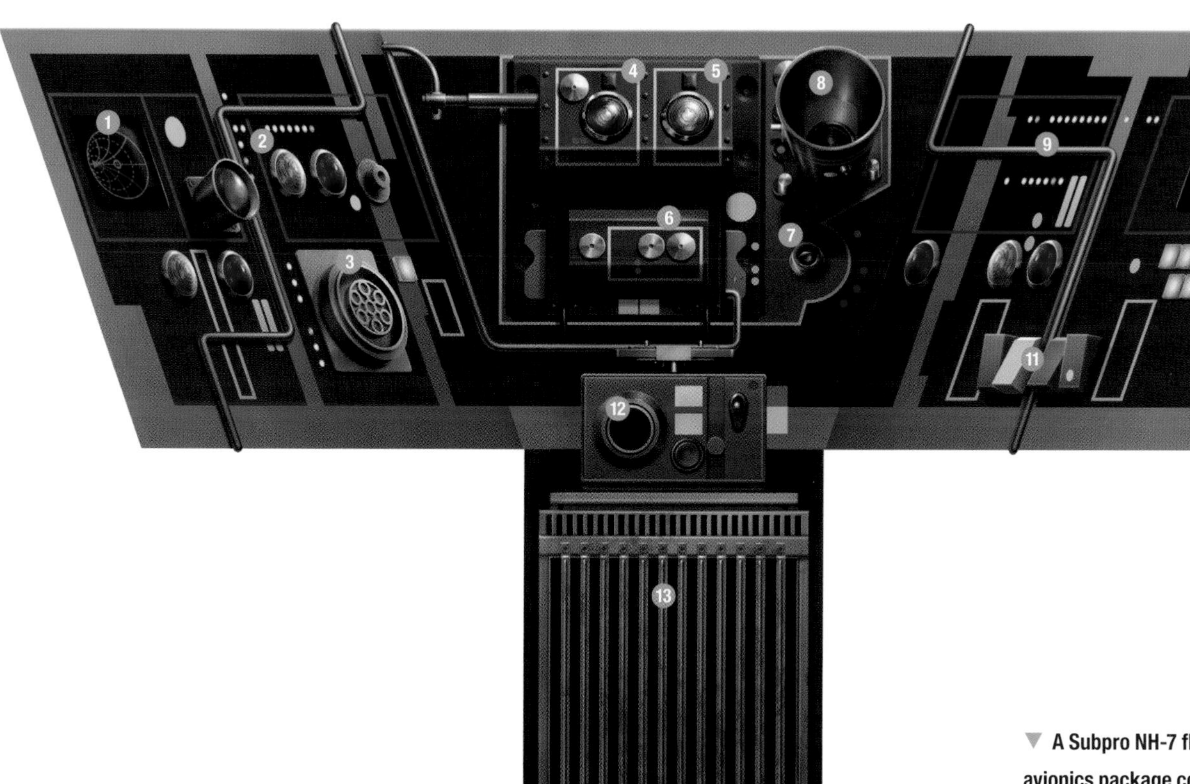

▼ A Subpro NH-7 flight control avionics package controlled the Y-wing's hyperdrive, repulsorlift drive, and sublight systems.

To view targeting data readouts and tactical displays in the BTL-A4 Y-wing, a rebel pilot utilized an extendable targeting computer screen mask with a targeting scope. The BTL-A4 Y-wing's targeting system consisted of a Fabritech ANc 2.7 tracking computer linked with a Fabritech SI 5g7 "Quickscan" imaging system. The computer drew data from the Y-wing's sensor systems, which included three additional Fabritech components: an ANs-5d lock track full-spectrum transceiver, a PTSA #PA-9r long-range phased tachyon detection array, and a PTAG #PG-7u short-range primary threat analysis grid. No matter how fast the Y-wing was traveling, the combination of sensors and computer systems provided the pilot with pinpoint-accurate targeting data.

BTL-A4 Y-WING HYPERDRIVE

Koensayr Manufacturing released the BTL-A4 Y-wing starfighter with a Class 1 hyperdrive equipped with a Koensayr R300-H hyperdrive motivator. A standard component of starships, hyperdrives enable ships to travel faster than the speed of light, and to jump into hyperspace, a dimension of space-time that is coterminous with realspace, also called normal space. Large objects in normal space cast "mass shadows" in hyperspace, so hyperspace jumps must be precisely calculated to avoid collisions. Hyperdrives utilize supra light "hypermatter" particles that form a field around the ship and allow a jump to lightspeed without changing the ship's complex mass/energy configuration. The hyperdrive field, once generated, must project around the ship for the duration of the journey to enable the ship to remain in hyperspace. A drive system failure will result in the ship dropping out of hyperspace and into realspace, in a potentially dangerous location, such as an asteroid belt or the heart of a star.

To ensure that a ship doesn't smash into a planet or star while traveling through hyperspace, pilots use astrogation computers to calculate routes and trajectories for their destinations. Due to size restrictions, most small starfighters use either astrogation computers or droids that contain data for only one hyperspace jump at a time. The Rebel Alliance Y-wing could hold coordinates for up to ten hyperspace jumps without being reprogrammed. Rebel technicians also utilized the Koensayr R300-H hyperdrive motivator for some Incom X-wing starfighters.

▲ **A member of Gray Squadron, the rebel pilot Lieutenant Gureni Telsij flew a BTL-A4 Y-wing at the Battle of Endor.**

◀ **Protected by the hyperdrive-generated invisible field of hypermatter particles, a stripped-down Y-wing travels across hyperspace.**

KOENSAYR R300-H HYPERDRIVE UNIT

1. Mounting frame
2. Energizer housing
3. Carry handle
4. Coaxium-lined reaction chamber
5. Swapable charge planes
6. Maintenance access panel
7. Secondary processor interface panel
8. Data lines from navigation unit
9. Cooling plate
10. Energizer coolant lines
11. Horizontal booster power lines
12. Field stabilizer
13. Power conduits

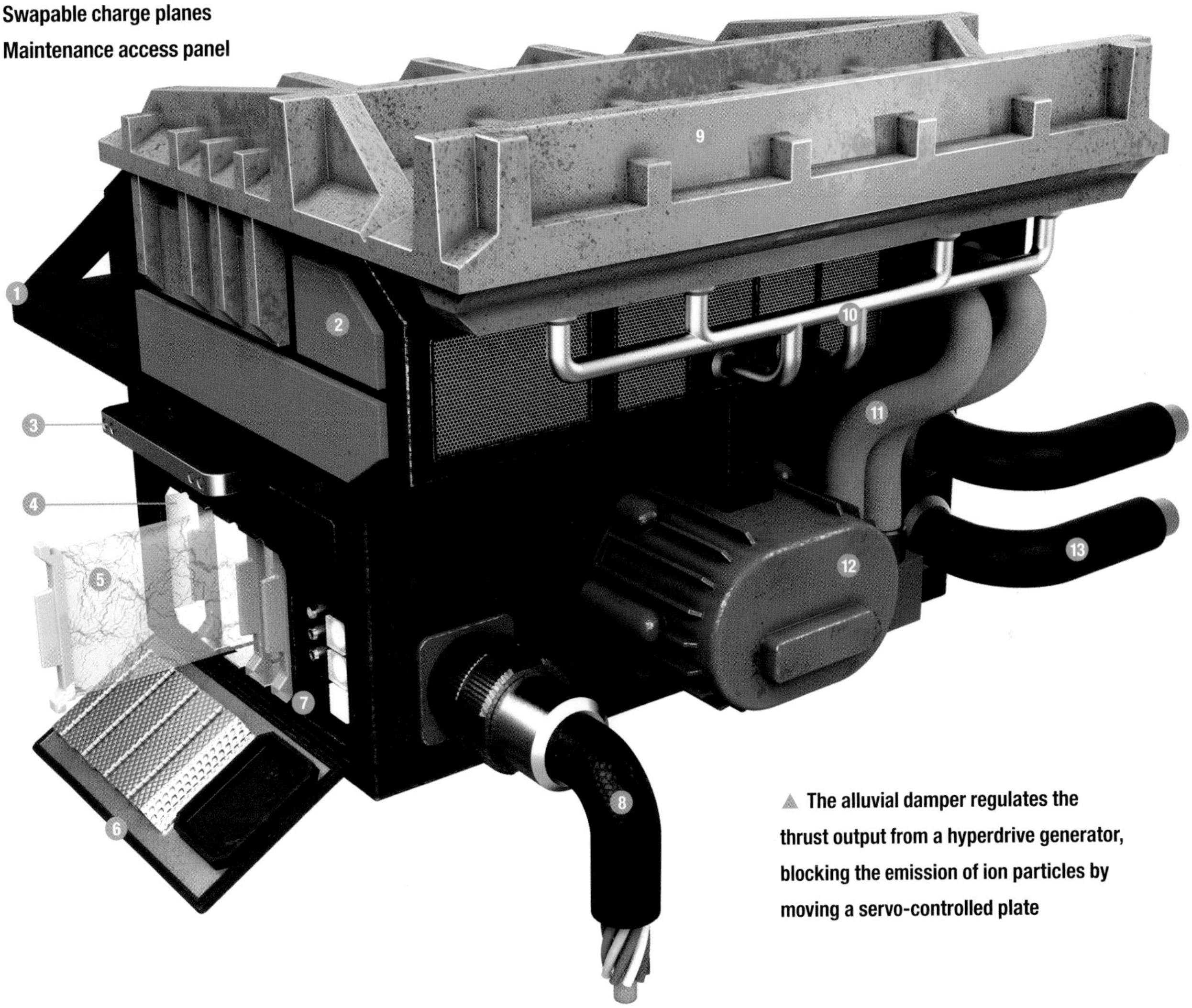

▲ The alluvial damper regulates the thrust output from a hyperdrive generator, blocking the emission of ion particles by moving a servo-controlled plate

▶ A hyperdrive subsystem, the horizontal booster provided energy to the ionization chamber to facilitate ignition.

BTL-A4 Y-WING WEAPONS AND DEFENSES

The BTL Y-wing's primary weapons were twin forward-firing Taim & Bak IX4 laser cannons, which were housed in a recessed slot at the front of the cockpit module, and boresighted to the Y-wing's flight path. A Novaldex power generator in the Y-wing's central spar fed energy to the laser cannons. Taim & Bak also manufactured KX5 laser cannons, which featured magnetic flashback suppressors, as an alternative to the short-barreled IX4s. Both the IX4s and KX5s were fire-linked, enabling a pilot to fire the cannons separately or both at the same time.

The Y-wing's standard secondary weapon was a turret-mounted, paired set of ArMek SW-4 ion cannons. The cannons fired ionized energy designed to overload a target's

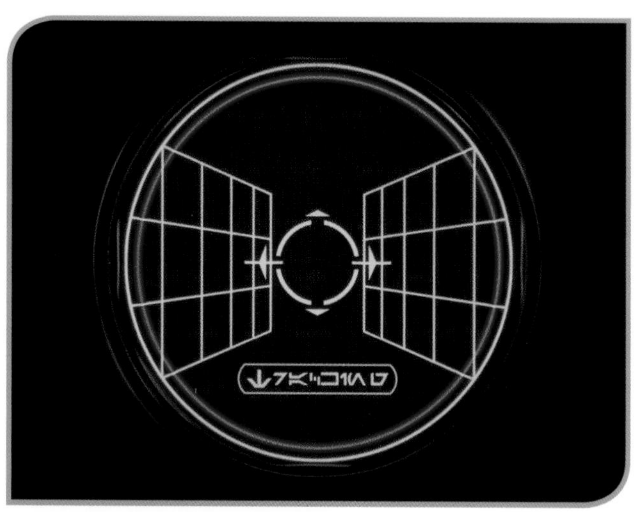

▲ The Y-wing's Fabritech SI 5g7 "Quickscan" imaging system displayed targeting data for moving or stationary targets.

◀ The Y-wing fired proton torpedoes, high-speed projectile weapons that released a wave of high-energy proton particles on impact.

Y-WING CANNONS

1. Twin ion cannons
2. Gunner
3. Proton torpedo racks
4. Arming power shell
5. Torpedo launch tube
6. Proton warhead
7. Pilot
8. Laser generator heat sink
9. Main laser coolant pump
10. Cooling coils
11. Forward laser coolant pump
12. Laser tip

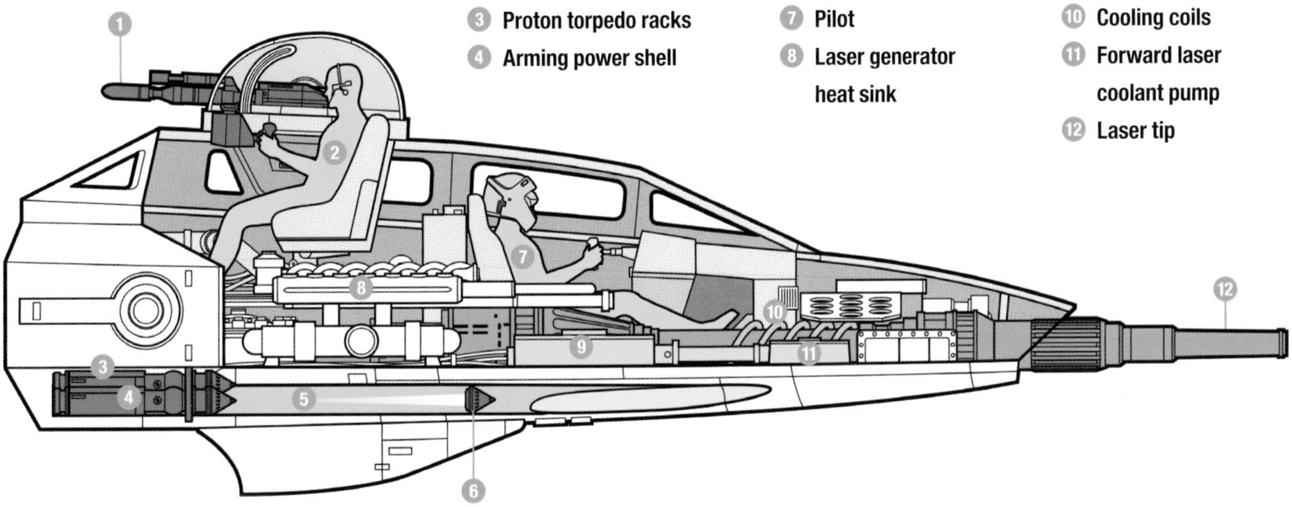

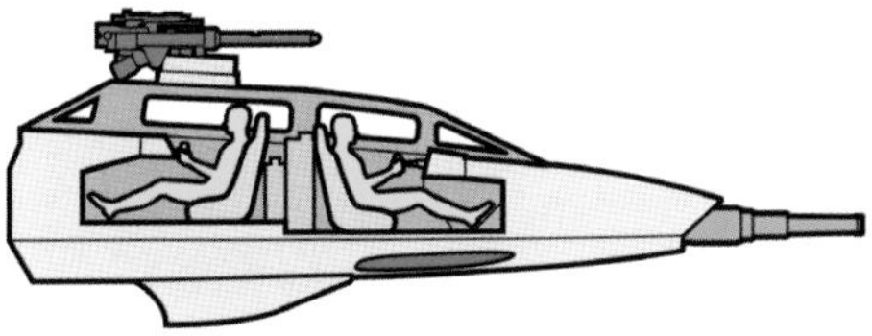

REAR FACING GUNNER

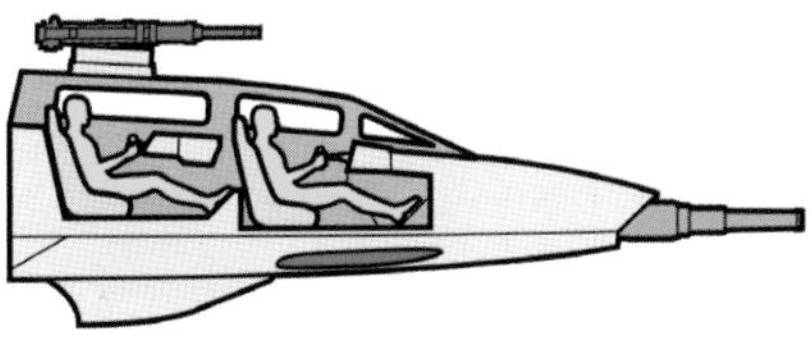

FORWARD FACING GUNNER

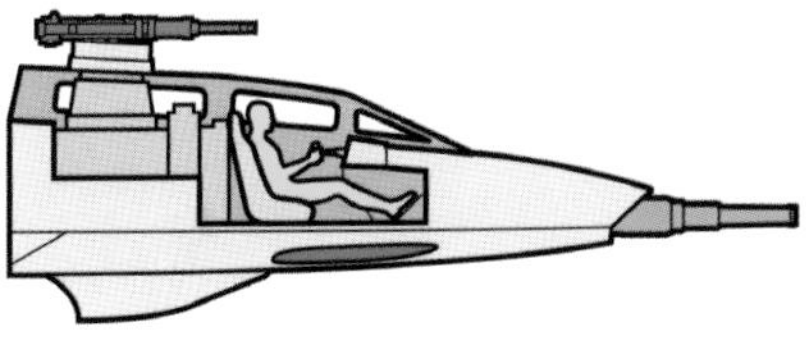

AUTOMATED TURRET

electronic systems. For the single-seat BTL-A4 Y-wing, the pilot, before flight, set the cannons' firing position in one of four fire arcs, and operated the cannons; in the two-seat BTL-S3, the tailgunner operated the cannons.

Rebel Alliance technicians replaced the Y-wing's two original six-torpedo magazines with lighter and more compact four-torpedo magazines that fed into a pair of Arakyd Flex Tube proton torpedo launchers. The Flex Tube launchers could fire a variety of ordnance, including proton torpedoes, concussion missiles, proton bombs, and cluster missiles.

The Y-wing's twin Koensayr R200 ion fission engines powered a Chempat deflector shield generator, which was located behind the Novaldex power generator, and linked to Chempat shield projectors. The pilot or astromech could angle the shields for maximum protection, or to cover damaged sections of the fighter.

▼ **The Krupx MG7 proton torpedo featured guidance computers and was generally used to soften targets for strafing runs but it could also take out key targets such as engines and shield generators.**

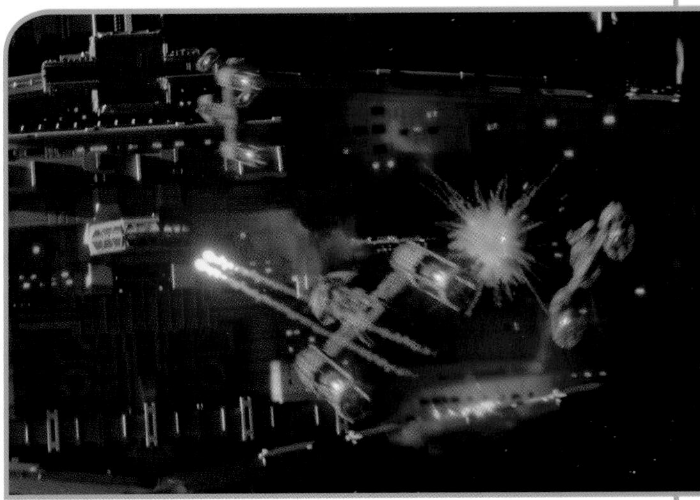

RZ-1 A-WING INTERCEPTOR

In the waning years of the Old Republic, Jedi peacekeepers realized they had need for a short-range starfighter that would complement a Jedi pilot's extraordinary reflexes and inherent skills. The Jedi Council commissioned Kuat Systems Engineering, a starship-manufacturing subsidiary of Kuat Drive Yards, to build the new craft. The result was the Delta-7 *Aethersprite*-class light interceptor also known as the Delta-7 "Jedi starfighter." Shaped like a sleek arrowhead, the Delta-7 achieved exceptional speed and agility by linking two Novaldex J-44 "Jetforce" sublight engines to two electromagnetic thrust nozzles, which focused and timed engine bursts to match the Jedi pilot's expert and exacting control of the fighter.

The Delta-7 served the Jedi until the end of the Clone Wars, which also brought an end to the Jedi Order. Because Kuat Systems Engineering executives knew the Delta-7 was, for non-Jedi pilots, almost overwhelmingly difficult to operate, the manufacturer soon ended production. Kuat began developing a starfighter prototype, the wedge-shaped R-22 A-wing, which they presented to the nascent Imperial Navy for consideration. Although the R-22 prototypes preformed admirably, the Navy had by then already contracted Sienar Fleet Systems to begin production of the Imperial TIE fighter, and would not grant permission for Kuat to mass-produce the R-22. Kuat sold the prototypes to the kingdom of Tammuz-an, which used the crafts to complement the Tammuz-an planetary defense fleet. Because the R-22 resembled a Tammuz-an ceremonial spear, the new owners dubbed the fighters Spearheads.

More than a decade later, rebel cells procured a number of Spearheads, which they transformed into the Rebel Fleet's fastest starfighter: the RZ-1 A-wing interceptor.

—Excerpt from *Official History of the Rebel Movements*, Volume One

◀ Rebel pilots, well aware that their modified RZ-1 A-wing starfighters were as incredibly fast as they were challenging to control, assisted their allies by flying directly into the second Death Star's superstructure at the Battle of Endor.

RZ-1 A-WING INTERCEPTOR

When the Tammuz-an purchased Kuat Systems Engineering R-22 starfighter prototypes for their planetary defense fleet, the prototypes came with two different cockpit configurations: one for a single pilot, and one with tandem seats for a pilot and passenger. Tammuz-an mechanics modified the prototypes' cockpits to accommodate the tall frames and long legs of Tammuz-an pilots. Subsequently, when the Rebel Alliance obtained used R-22s, their first task was to adjust the flight controls and refit the cockpits with seats suitable for standard-height humanoids. Rebels also modified the two-seat R-22 for use as a pilot-training starfighter.

In the process of refitting the R-22 cockpits, engineers examined other sections of the craft to determine necessary modifications and upgrades, preferably using parts already at their disposal. Because Kuat produced the R-22 as a small, short-range fighter without a hyperdrive, and because the Rebel Fleet was in desperate need for more hyperdrive-equipped fighters, the rebel engineers' next task was to make space within the fuselage for a hyperdrive generator.

▲ **Kuat Systems Engineering incorporated aspects of their Delta-7 *Aethersprite*-class light interceptor, a two-engine short-range fighter designed for Jedi pilots, for the R-22 prototype.**

▼ **The pilots of Phoenix Squadron, a cell of resistance fighters, jumped down from catwalks and into the waiting cockpits of their RZ-1 interceptors.**

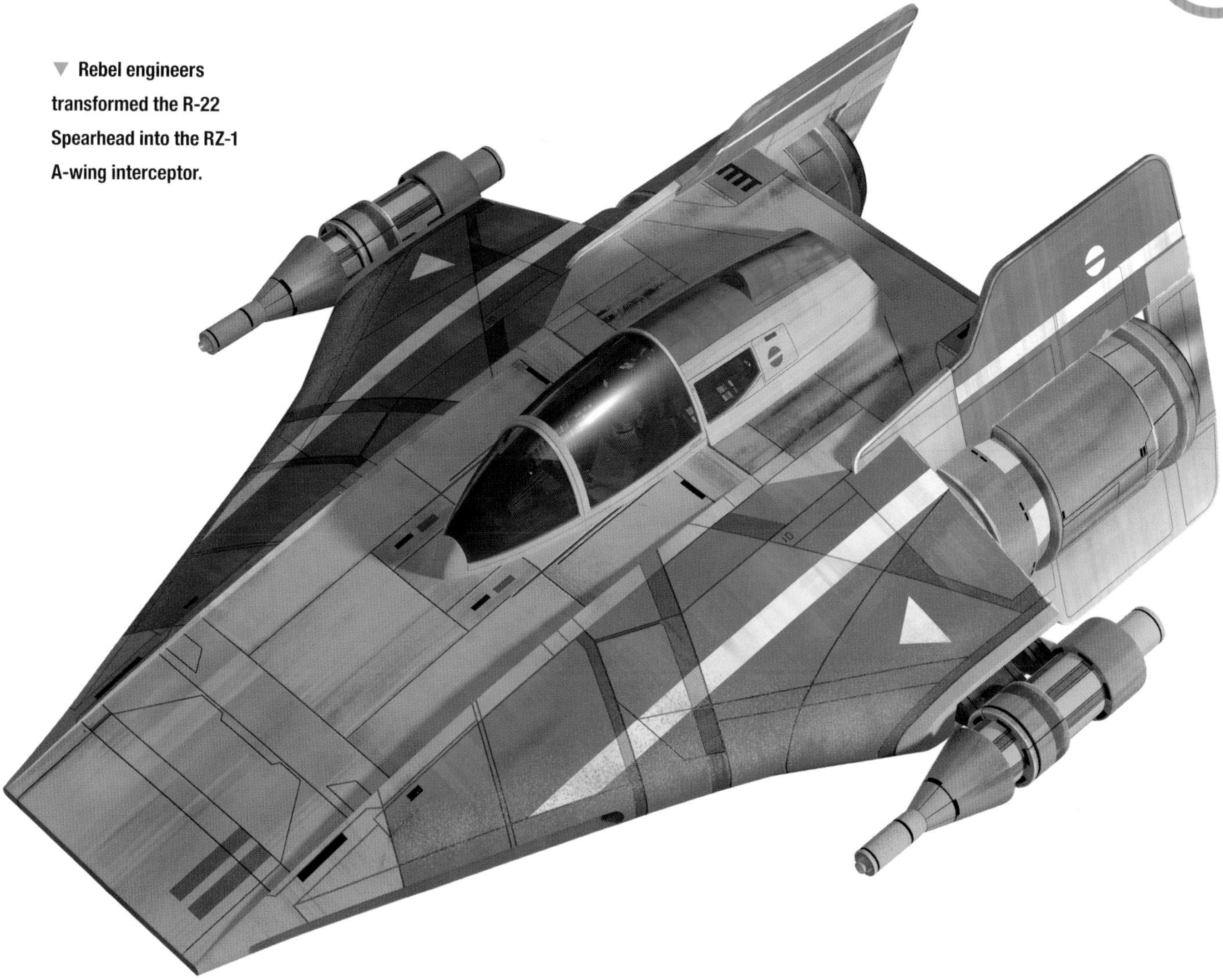

▼ **Rebel engineers transformed the R-22 Spearhead into the RZ-1 A-wing interceptor.**

Reportedly, the engineers considered installing an integrated astromech droid before they realized that the R-22's lightweight frame was durable enough to carry two giant Novaldex J-77 "Event Horizon" sublight engines—the fastest engines available—without buckling under their torque. Engineers also determined that by omitting an integrated astromech, they could better utilize the frame's limited available space for speed-boosting technology and advanced weapons and defensive systems. Finding more opportunities for improvement, the rebels continued working on the A-wing.

▶ **Prior to the official foundation of the Alliance to Restore the Republic, Phoenix Squadron launched their A-wings from the command ship *Phoenix Home* to attack Imperial targets.**

The addition of Novaldex J-77 "Event Horizon" sublight engines to the R-22 prototypes resulted in a fighter that outperformed the Empire's fastest production-model starfighter, the TIE/in Interceptor. To further increase acceleration and speed, rebel mechanics swapped out the R-22's original hull armor, heavy weapons, and deflector shield systems with lighter-weight materials and technology. In test flights, rebels determined that the craft was ideally suited to hit-and-run missions, surgical strikes on capital ships, long-range patrols, and reconnaissance and intelligence-gathering missions. Pilots also noted that the craft's twin stabilizers and control surfaces enabled it to operate effectively as an atmospheric fighter.

Rebels designated their modified fighter the RZ-1 A-wing. Despite the fighter's incredible speed, critics noted that the craft was essentially a cockpit attached to two extremely powerful engines, and that even a pilot with Jedi-like reflexes might have had difficulty maneuvering the RZ-1 without assistance from an astromech unit. As a result, rebel commanders allowed only their most skilled and accomplished pilots to fly the A-wings.

Another conditional requirement for assignments to fly an A-wing was that the pilot had a compact physique. Although rebel crews had done their best to modify the cockpit and controls for standard-sized humanoids, many pilots discovered that the A-wing cockpit was unusually cramped. After the fall of the Empire, the New Republic commissioned Kuat Systems Engineering to produce A-wings with cockpits that were more accommodating to pilots of different sizes.

▲ **RZ-1 A-wings sometimes trailed behind other ships in the Rebel Fleet to trick enemy pilots into thinking the A-wing was a slower starfighter.**

◀ **RZ-1 A-wing interceptors made up the starfighters of Green Squadron, which served Rebel Alliance at the Battle of Endor during the Galactic Civil War.**

▼ One of the fastest starfighters in the galaxy, the RZ-1 A-wing did not have an onboard astromech droid, and was extremely challenging for pilots to control.

▼ RZ-1 A-wings followed X-wing starfighters and diverted their TIE fighter pursuers during a daring mission to destroy the second Death Star.

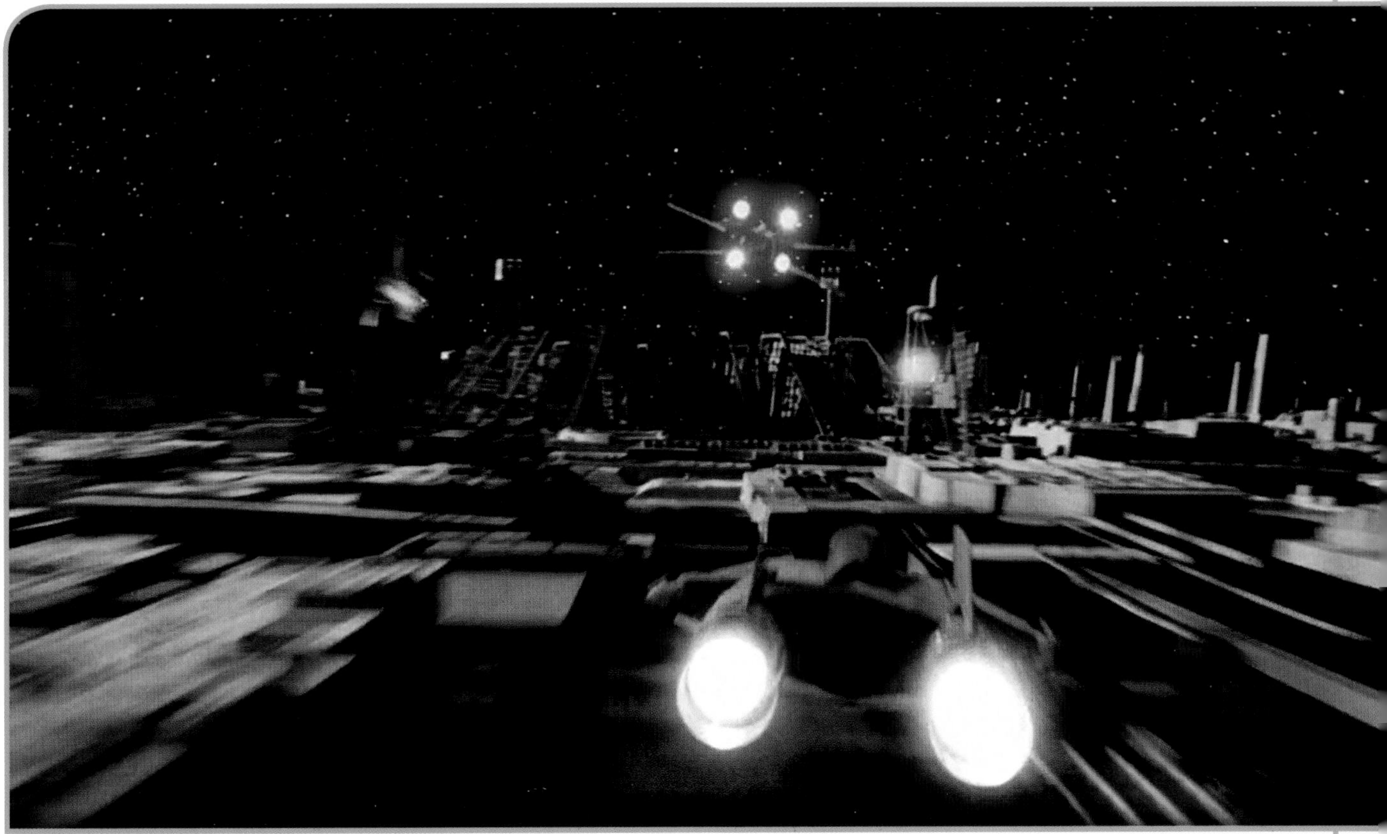

SPECIFICATIONS RZ-1 A-WING INTERCEPTOR

MANUFACTURER: Kuat Systems Engineering
AFFILIATION: Alliance to Restore the Republic, New Republic
MODEL: RZ-1 A-wing interceptor
CLASS: Starfighter
LENGTH: 6.9 m (22 ft 8 in)
WIDTH: 4.47 m (14 ft 8 in)
HEIGHT: 2.47 m (8 ft 1in)
MAXIMUM ACCELERATION: 5,100 G
MEGALIGHT PER HOUR: 120 MGLT
MAXIMUM SPEED (ATMOSPHERE): 1,300 kph
ENGINE: Novaldex J-77 "Event Horizon" sublight engines (2)
HYPERDRIVE: Class 1; Incom GBk-785 hyperdrive motivators (2)
SHIELDING: Sirplex Z-9 deflector shield projector
NAVIGATION SYSTEM: Microaxial LpL-449 navigation computer (2 jump limit)
TARGETING SYSTEMS: Fabritech ANq 3.6 tracking computer; IN-344-B "Sightline" holographic imaging system
ARMAMENT: Borstel RG-9 laser cannons (2); Dymek HM-6 concussion missile launchers (2); concussion missiles (12)
ESCAPE CRAFT: Ejector seat
CREW: Pilot (1)
LIFE SUPPORT: Equipped
CONSUMABLES: 1 week
COST: 175,000 credits new; 90,000 credits used

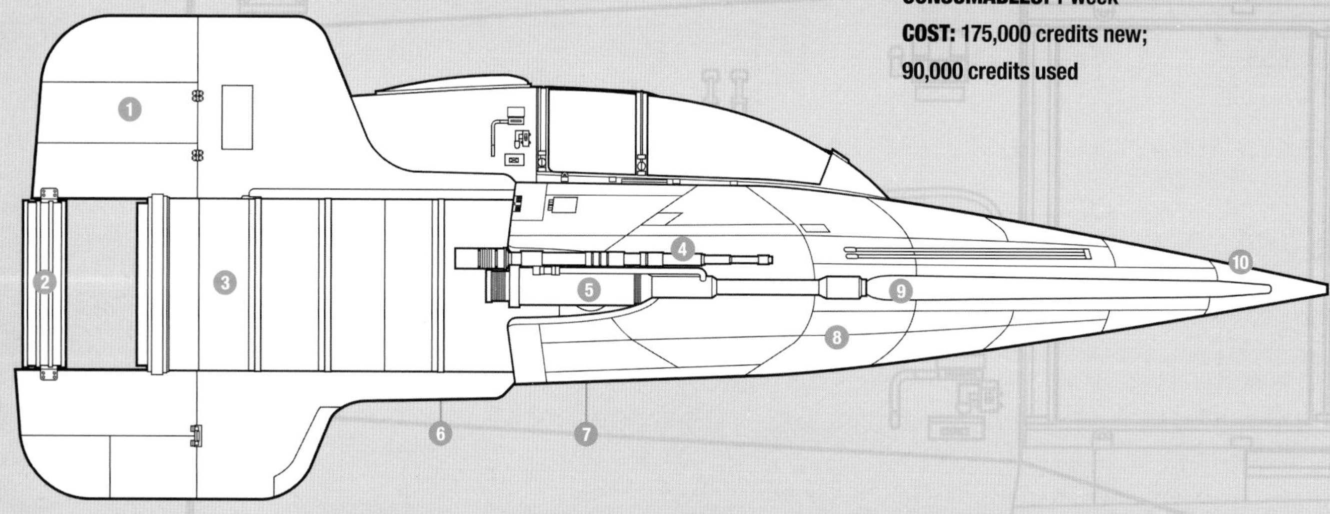

1. Adjustable stabilizers
2. Thrust vector control
3. Sublight engine
4. Low-power targeting laser
5. Laser cannon
6. Fusion reactor
7. Hyperdrive
8. Concussion-missile magazine
9. Missile launch tube
10. Reinforced front wedge
11. Thrust control jets
12. Fusion reactor exhaust
13. Laser cannon swivel mounting
14. Gyro-stabilizing unit (concealed)
15. Deflector shield generator
16. Deflector shield projector
17. Emergency datalog
18. Multi-spectral holographic imager (concealed)
19. Cockpit canopy
20. Sensor power-jamming array
21. Maintenance access hatch
22. Targeting computer system
23. Forward sensor array
24. Towing slot

▶ Rebel mechanics installed dual MPS Bpr-99 fusion reactors to power the A-wing's Novaldex J-77 sublight engines, and linked two Incom GBK-785 hyperdrive motivators to engage both engine nacelles to make the jump to lightspeed.

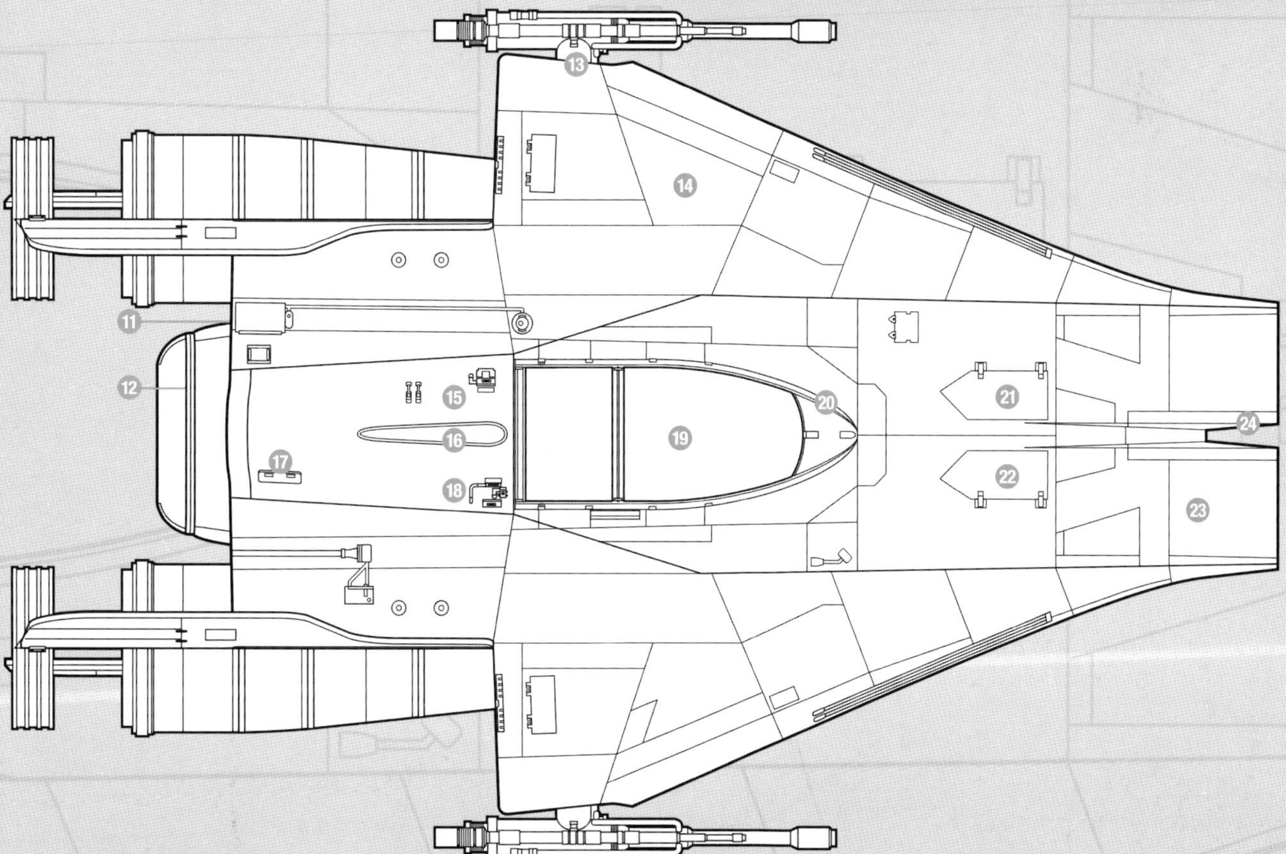

▲ The RZ-1 A-wing carried only two standard Borstel Galactic Defense RG-9 laser cannons, but a unique swivel-mounting system greatly enhanced the fighter's combat effectiveness. A short hydro-servo bearing at the end of each wing tip allowed both cannons to rotate and fire in a 120° arc (60° above and below the horizontal).

VIEWS

FRONT 3/4 VIEW

Like its R-22 prototype predecessor, the RZ-1 A-wing was without an astromech droid. The A-wing's navicomputer could carry hyperspace coordinates for two lightspeed jumps, and could also receive ally-transmitted coordinates for emergency jumps.

PORT VIEW

The A-wing's wedge-shaped design and explosive fuels system could cause tremendous damage when the craft collided with another ship, but at the cost of the A-wing pilot's life unless the pilot could eject.

DORSAL AND VENTRAL VIEWS

Lightweight durasteel plates covered the A-wing's titanium alloy frame. A Sirplex Z-9 deflector shield projector, positioned directly behind the cockpit canopy, projected a layer of ray shielding from prow to stern.

FORWARD AND AFT VIEWS

Rebel technicians modified some A-wing cannons to pivot and rotate 360º, enabling the pilot to shoot straight back while racing forward. However, pilots soon realized that the cannons' swivel mounts were prone to jamming, especially when the cannons fired at targets directly behind the craft. Even after engineers identified and replaced the swivel mounts' problematic components, the A-wing still required more post-flight maintenance checks than other rebel starfighters.

RZ-1 A-WING COCKPIT AND FLIGHT CONTROLS

As Imperial Academy defectors joined the Rebel Alliance, it's not surprising that some rebel pilots noted that the A-wing's lightweight frame offered a freedom of manual control comparable to that in Imperial TIE fighters, albeit within a remarkably cramped cockpit. A combination of adjustable thrust-vector controls built into each engine and thruster-control jets located between the A-wing's engines supplied the craft's famed maneuverability. During atmospheric flight, pilots controlled the A-wing's flight path by making small adjustments to the stabilizer wings.

Kuat Systems Engineering built the original R-22 prototype's pressurized cockpit with a transparisteel canopy that was hinged to lift and tilt back to allow egress for the pilot. The pilot could lower the canopy manually or program it to lower automatically before launch. After rebel cells obtained the R-22 prototypes, engineers retrofitted some crafts with canopies that slid on tracks to open and shut. Although some pilots preferred the track system, mechanics soon determined the hinged canopy was easier to maintain and less likely to malfunction.

The RZ-1 A-wing's internal systems included a Fabritech IN-344-B "Sightline" holographic imager, a Microaxial LpL-449 flight controller, and a Fabritech ANq 3.6 targeting computer. Because learning to fly an A-wing posed challenges for even experienced starpilots, rebel engineers and technicians constructed a basic training version, the RZ-1T A-wing, which pilots used to practice maneuvers. The RZ-1T's cockpit housed two tandem seats, with the front seat for the pilot and the rear seat for the flight instructor.

◀ Using multi-spectral imagers and other sensors, rebel A-wing pilots could gather information and escape back into hyperspace before Imperial TIE fighter pilots could scramble or pursue.

RZ-1T A-WING CONTROLS

1. Targeting display
2. Ship status display
3. Weapon status display
4. Power management
5. Sensor display
6. Accelerometer
7. Velocity indicator
8. Attitude indicator
9. Environment scanners
10. Air circulators
11. Communications
12. Air scrubbers
13. Annunciator panel
14. Warning lights
15. Life support controls

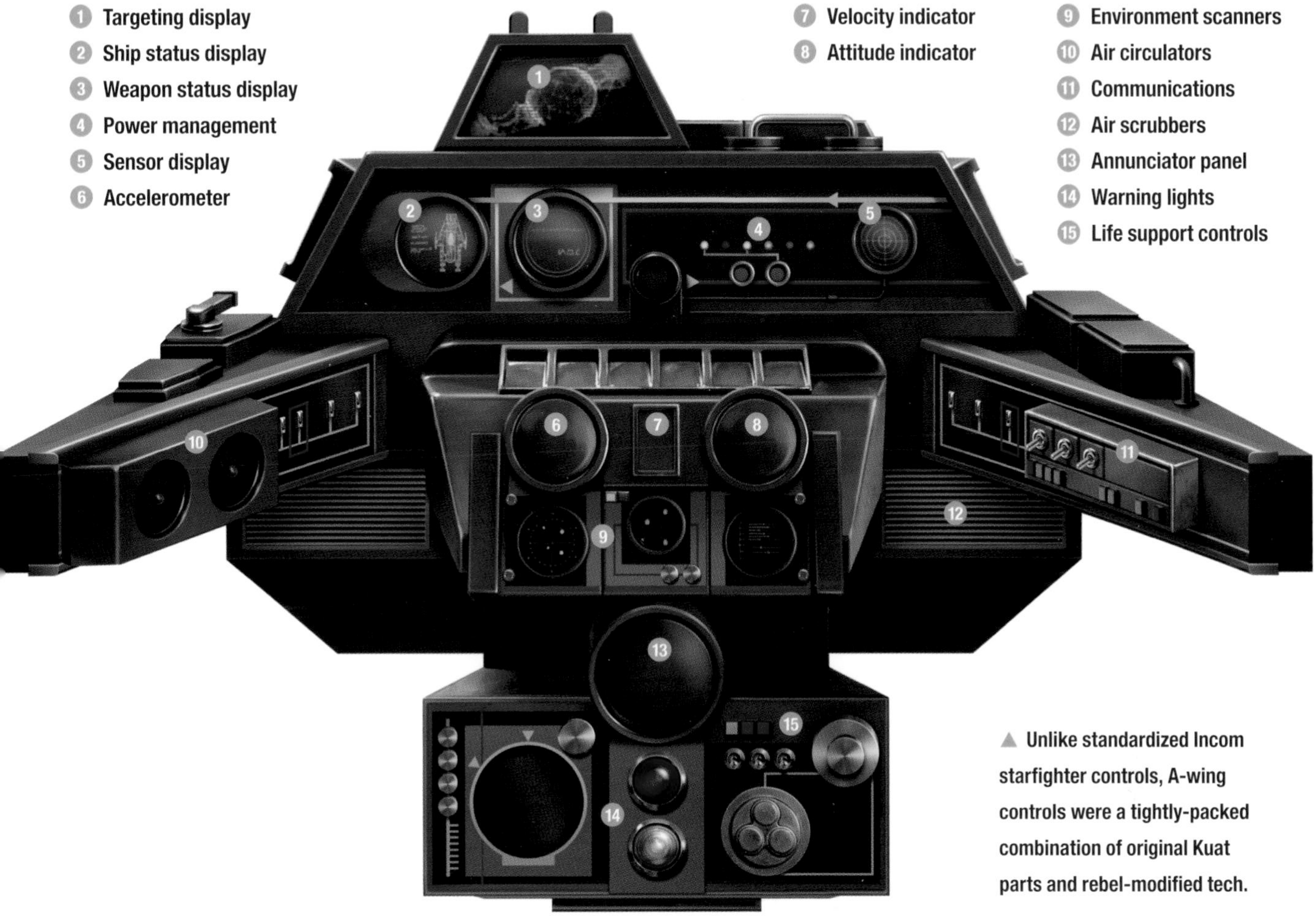

▲ Unlike standardized Incom starfighter controls, A-wing controls were a tightly-packed combination of original Kuat parts and rebel-modified tech.

▶ A former Z-95 Headhunter pilot for a Thyferran batca cartel, Rebel Commander Arvel Crynyd served with Green Squadron. After Imperial laserfire severely damaged Crynyd's A-wing, the doomed pilot crashed his craft into the Super Star Destroyer *Executor*'s bridge tower, a sacrifice that resulted in a massive explosion that helped destroy the *Executor*.

A/SF-01 B-WING STARFIGHTER

Classified Communique
To: Alliance High Command
From: General Carlist Rieekan

Three hours ago, Admiral Ackbar and I watched a test flight of a new starfighter. It's a single-pilot craft, hyperdrive equipped. To say the craft is well armed would be a massive understatement. To our knowledge, Ackbar and I believe this craft may be the most well armed starfighter in the galaxy.

It's also an unusual design, the product of a joint venture between a Mon Calamari engineer named Quarrie and the Verpine starship manufacturer Slayne & Korpil, which made fighters for the Republic Navy during the Clone Wars. Although the Verpine remain officially neutral in their political dealings with the Empire, their commitment to producing this new fighter is a strong indication that they support our Alliance. Slayne & Korpil's chief engineers repeatedly conveyed that the new fighter originated as a personal project for Quarrie, and that they couldn't have produced it without him. Quarrie developed an initial prototype as a blockade buster starfighter, and the Slayne & Korpil production model has that same classification. They've designated the new fighter the A/SF-01 B-Wing.

The B-wing supports an array of weapons including ion cannons, proton torpedo launchers, and laser cannons. Because the cockpit is surrounded by a unique gyro-stabilization system, the pilot always remains stationary, even as the rest of the ship rotates during flight. General Ackbar will confirm that the fighter's gyro-stabilization system and S-foil-mounted weapons systems present unique challenges for even our best pilots, but given that a single B-wing packs enough firepower to attack and destroy capital ships, the payoff will be well worth it.

Pilot selection and training begins immediately.

◀ Equipped with gyroscopic technology in defiance of conventional starfighter designs, the rebel B-wing trained its powerful energy weapons on large capital ships during the Battle of Endor while X-wings engaged Imperial TIE fighters.

B-WING ORIGINS

Prior to the Clone Wars, the insectoid Verpine shipwrights at starship manufacturer Slayn & Korpil produced the T-6 shuttle, an unarmed short-range vessel for the Jedi Order. The "Jedi ambassador shuttle" featured a rotating engine block and a conical, gyroscopic command module—housing a cockpit and cabin—that bisected the broad, semicircular wing that made up the shuttle's body. Shock-resistant gimbals, one of many technological advancements included in the shuttle by its Verpine designers, enabled the T-6's body to rotate around the command module while the cockpit remained level to a horizon or the plane of travel.

Slayn & Korpil subsequently produced the V-19 Torrent starfighter and the H-60 Tempest bomber for the Republic Navy. The V-19 Torrent had port and starboard S-foils, or moveable wings, that were tipped with laser cannons, and also a third pivoting central S-foil positioned behind cockpit. The H-60 Tempest's body was essentially a broad, rigid airfoil with detachable cockpits—one for a pilot, one for a gunner—attached to each end. The Navy disliked the H-60's design, but the V-19 saw action in many conflicts against Separatist forces.

Fifteen years after the foundation of Galactic Empire, on the planet Shantipole, the reclusive Mon Calamari engineer Quarrie sought to improve on Verpine designs to create a new starfighter. Quarrie incorporated aspects from the T-6 shuttle, V-19 starfighter, and H-60 bomber into a prototype, the B6 starfighter, also known as the Blade Wing.

◀ **In its landing configuration, the T-6 shuttle's command module and wing aligned horizontally. In flight mode, the wing rotated 90° to align vertically with the command module.**

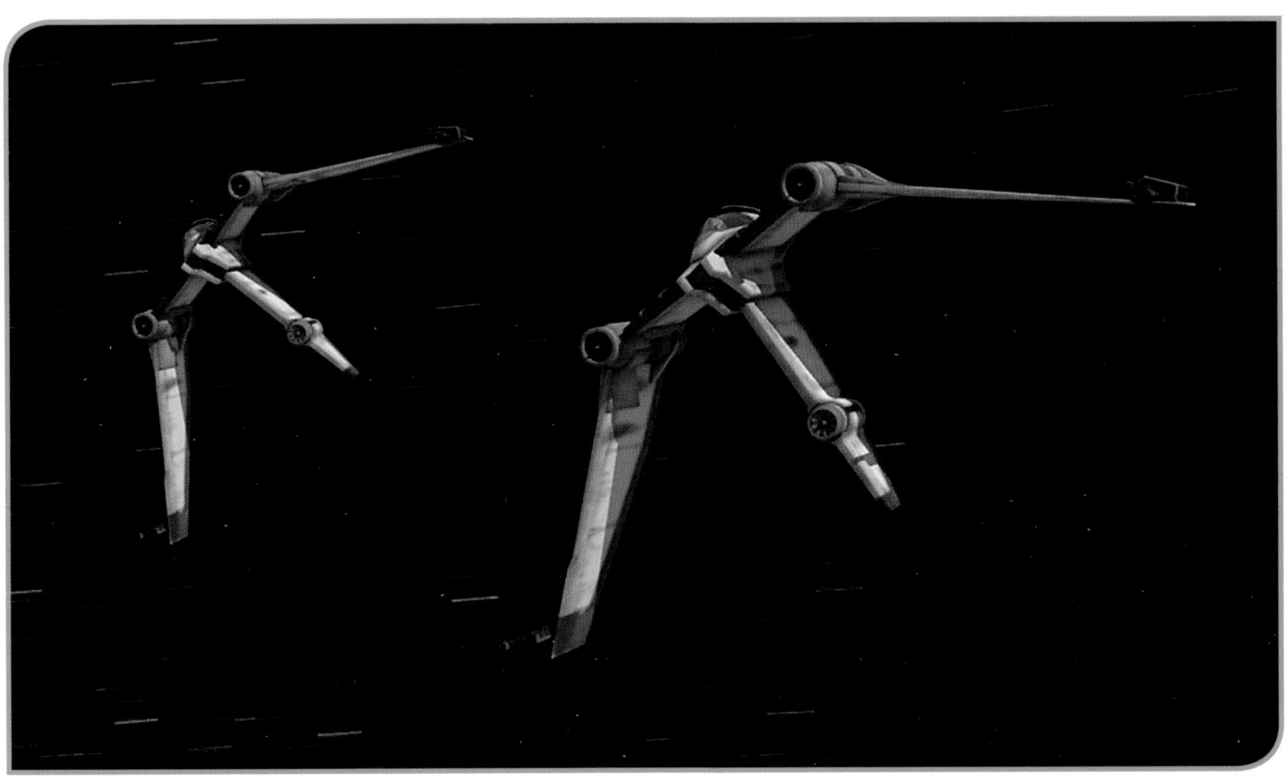

▲ Early models of the V-19 Torrent starfighter used an external hyperdrive ring while later models packed a built-in Class 1 hyperdrive.

▼ Although Republic Navy officials initially approved Slayn & Korpil's schematics for the H-60 Tempest bomber, the craft's two separate-purposed cockpits proved problematic for clone trooper test pilots, and most H-60s wound up in scrap yards.

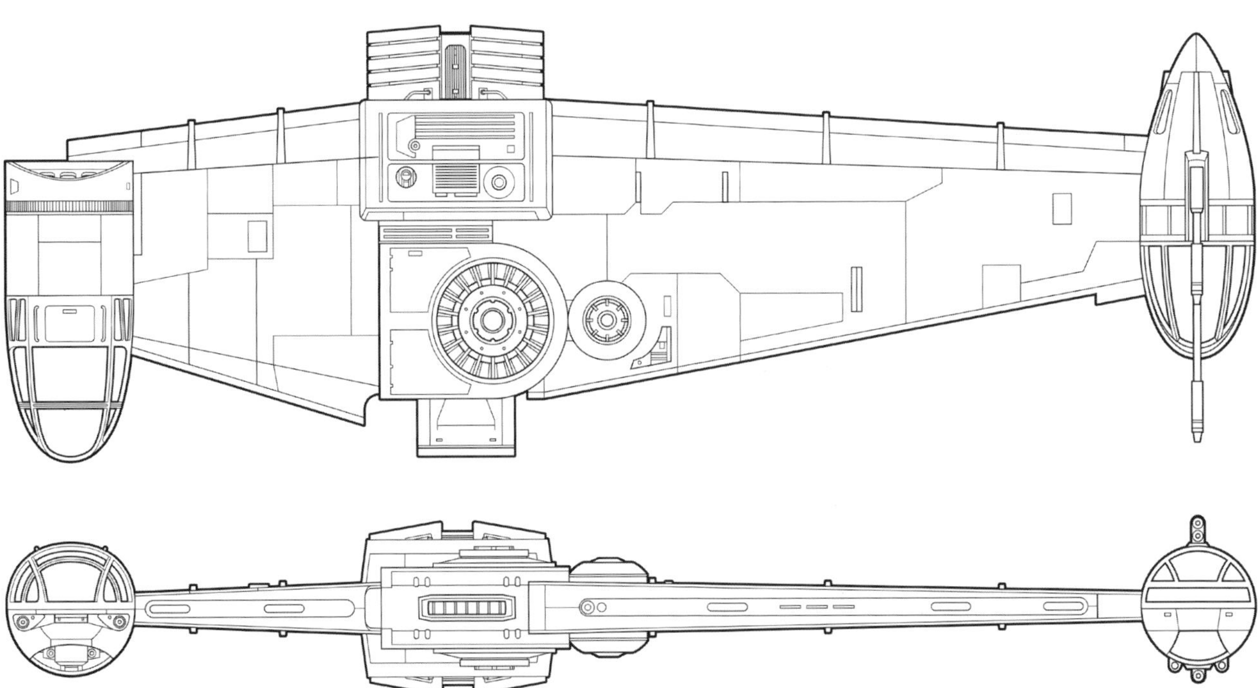

B6 PROTOTYPE – THE BLADE WING

While the Blade Wing bore a strong resemblance to the Slayn & Korpil H-60 Tempest bomber, it had a gyroscopic cockpit like the T-6 shuttle, and weapon-laden S-foils like the V-19 Torrent starfighter. The Blade Wing also boasted an outrigger with a gunner's turret, and a hyperdrive-powered composite-beam laser system, a highly destructive weapon that gave the prototype greater firepower than any other starfighter. Thanks to Quarrie, the prototype's creator, the Blade Wing enabled rebel agents to break through an Imperial blockade and deliver food and supplies to people on the planet Ibaar.

But because the Blade Wing's complex and costly multi-cannon firing system risked an energy drain that rendered the hyperdrive inoperable, the rebels knew a production run would present technical as well as financial challenges.

▶ **The rebel pilot Hera Syndulla steered the Blade Wing through its first test flight alongside untamed dactillions across the skies of Shantipole.**

▼ **Resting on a landing pad outside the engineer Quarrie's workshop on Shantipole, the prototype B6 starfighter Blade Wing's unusual appearance belied its formidable firepower.**

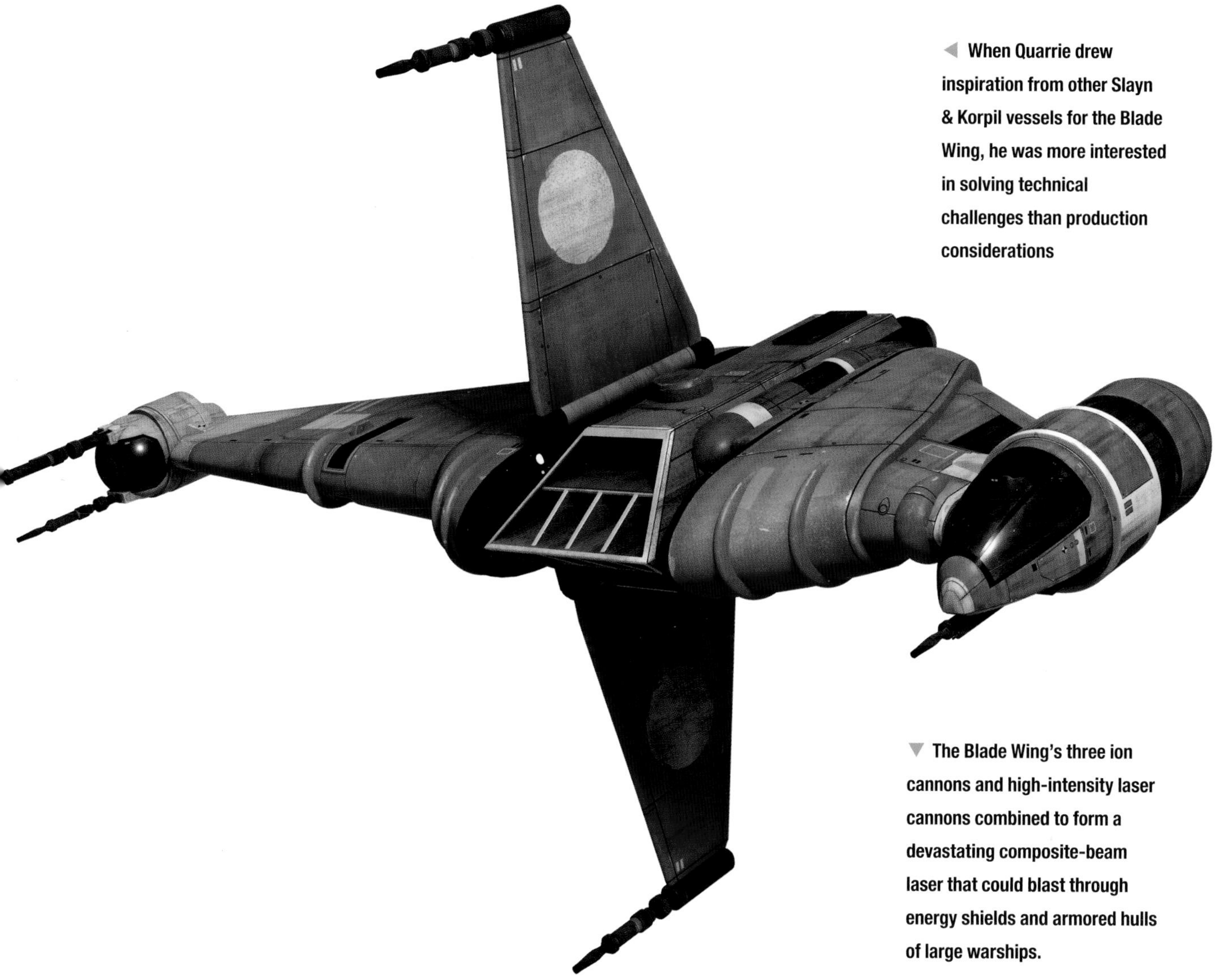

When Quarrie drew inspiration from other Slayn & Korpil vessels for the Blade Wing, he was more interested in solving technical challenges than production considerations

The Blade Wing's three ion cannons and high-intensity laser cannons combined to form a devastating composite-beam laser that could blast through energy shields and armored hulls of large warships.

Quarrie proposed to replace the gunner's turret with an automated weapons pod, a decision that would reduce costs considerably. He also agreed to allow the rebel and former Mandalorian warrior Sabine Wren to redesign the Blade Wing's targeting system and weapons package. Collaborating with the rebels, Quarrie used the prototype as a basis for a new starfighter: the A/SF-01 B-wing.

Fortunately, the influential rebel ally Senator Bail Organa of Alderaan, after learning that Quarrie used Slayn & Korpil parts and technology for the Blade Wing, convinced Verpine engineers at Slayn & Korpil to work with Quarrie to secretly build more "B-wings." Because Quarrie had begun work on his B-wing prototype on Shantipole, the Verpine respectfully named their collaborative worksite the Allied/Shantipole Facility.

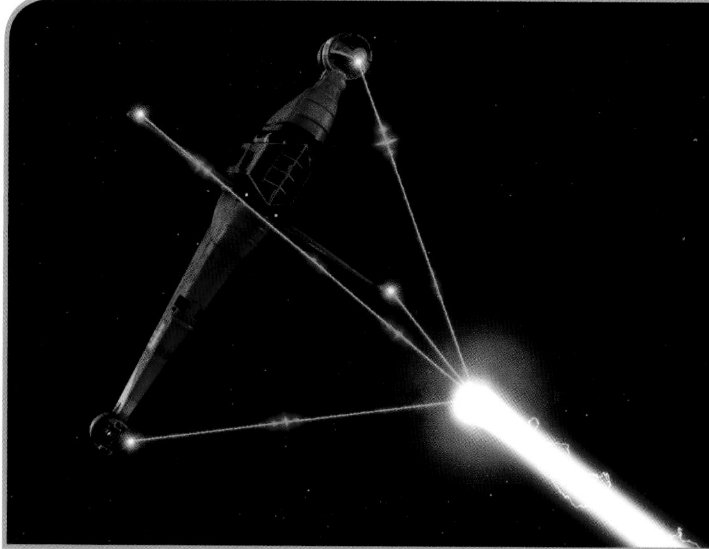

A/SF-01 B-WING STARFIGHTER

When the Rebel Alliance commissioned Slayn & Korpil to begin work on a new assault starfighter, the manufacturers' goal was to produce an affordable production model with the maneuverability and destructive power of the B6 prototype but without the prototype's maintenance problems. Although they succeeded in making the A/SF-01 B-wing less expensive than the B-6 prototype, and similarly maneuverable and powerful, the B-wing's technological complexity ensured that the craft would require more maintenance than other starfighters in the Alliance fleet.

The gyro-servos that kept the command pod in a fixed position were a mechanic's nightmare. Though well-built and durable, the gyro-servos underwent tremendous stress when used and failed if not in prime condition.

A failure could lock the wings in place, forcing the pilot to fly the craft in whatever wing configuration was current at the moment the servos failed. Because the B-wing relied on its gyroscopic stabilization to minimize g-stresses during combat maneuvers, servo-failure made tight turns and rapid maneuvers physically punishing for pilots.

The B-wing's single Quadex Kyromaster engine drove the large fighter in realspace. Four cooling vents, commonly called "intakes," on each side of a splitter plate dissipated engine and exhaust heat, but the fighter still emitted a fairly strong infrared image. The B-wing's maximum sublight speed was fairly low, but the shields were quite strong. Maintenance and stability concerns aside, the B-wing, at the time of its production, was most heavily-armed starfighter in the galaxy.

▶ The most heavily-armed starfighter in the rebel arsenal, the B-wing used a gyro-servo system that stabilized the command pod while the primary wing spun around it, which helped the pilot and fire-control sensors stay on target.

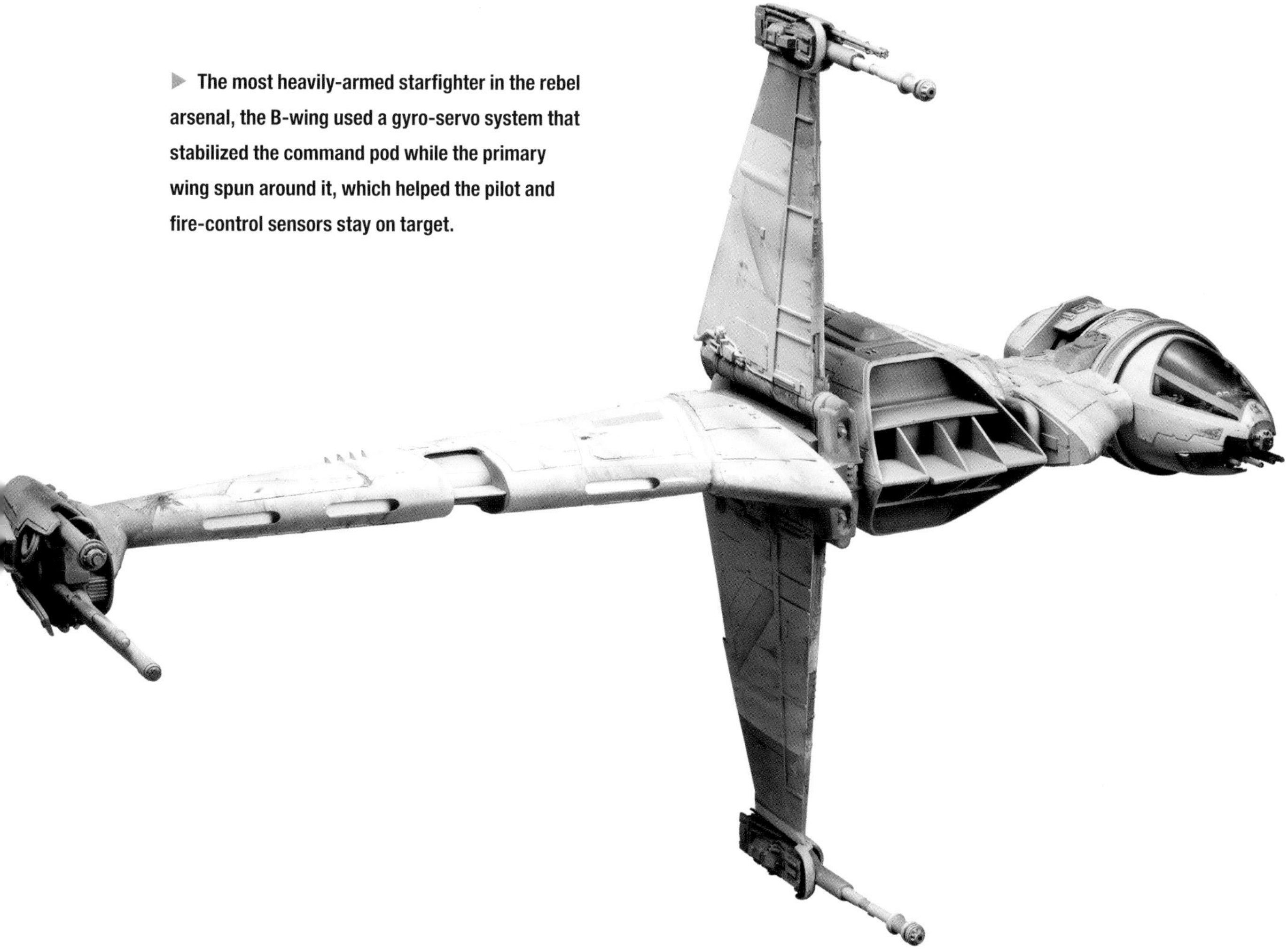

◀ B-wings helped the Rebel Alliance defeat the Imperial armada at the Battle of Endor.

▶ The Rebel Alliance used the B-wing primarily as an attack vessel against the Empire's capital ships, but also for escorting X- and Y-wing fighter squadrons and Alliance convoys.

SPECIFICATIONS A/SF-01 B-WING STARFIGHTER

MANUFACTURER: Slayn & Korpil
AFFILIATION: Alliance to Restore the Republic, New Republic
MODEL: A/SF-01 B-wing
CLASS: Heavy assault starfighter
LENGTH: 16.9m (55ft 5in)
WIDTH: 2.9m (9ft 6in)
HEIGHT: 2.5m (8ft 2in) (7.3m/23ft 11in with S-foils in attack position)
MAXIMUM ACCELERATION: 2,390 G
MEGALIGHT PER HOUR: 91 MGLT
MAXIMUM SPEED (ATMOSPHERE): 950 kph (590 mph)
ENGINE: Quadex Kyromaster engine with 4 thrusters

HYPERDRIVE: HYd-997 hyperdrive motivator
SHIELDING: Sirplex Zr-41 shield generator
NAVIGATION SYSTEM: Microaxial LpM-549 navigation computer
TARGETING SYSTEMS: Fabritech ANq 3.6 computer tracking computer
ARMAMENT: ArMek SW-7a ion cannons (3); Gyrhil R-9x laser cannons (1-4); Gyrhil 72 twin autoblaster (1); Krupx MG9 proton torpedo launchers (2); laser-guided bombs

ESCAPE CRAFT: Ejector seat
CREW: Pilot (1)
LIFE SUPPORT: Equipped
CONSUMABLES: 1 week
COST: 220,00 credits new; 120,000 used

▼ Although the B-wing had more powerful weapons than any other starfighter in the Rebel Fleet, it lacked the speed and maneuverability of the Y-wing, A-wing, and X-wing fighters.

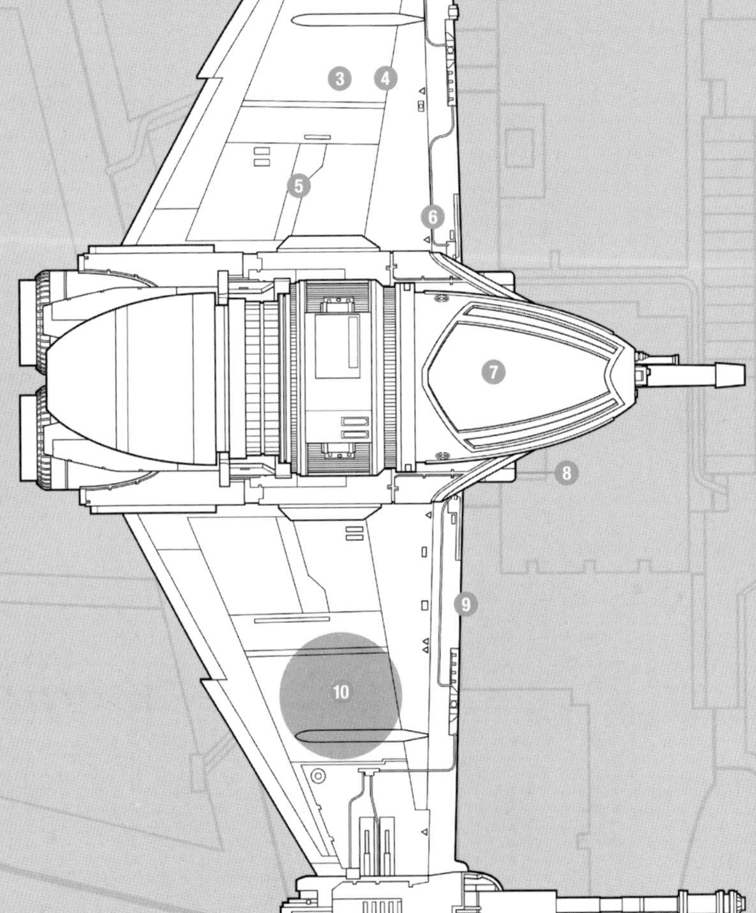

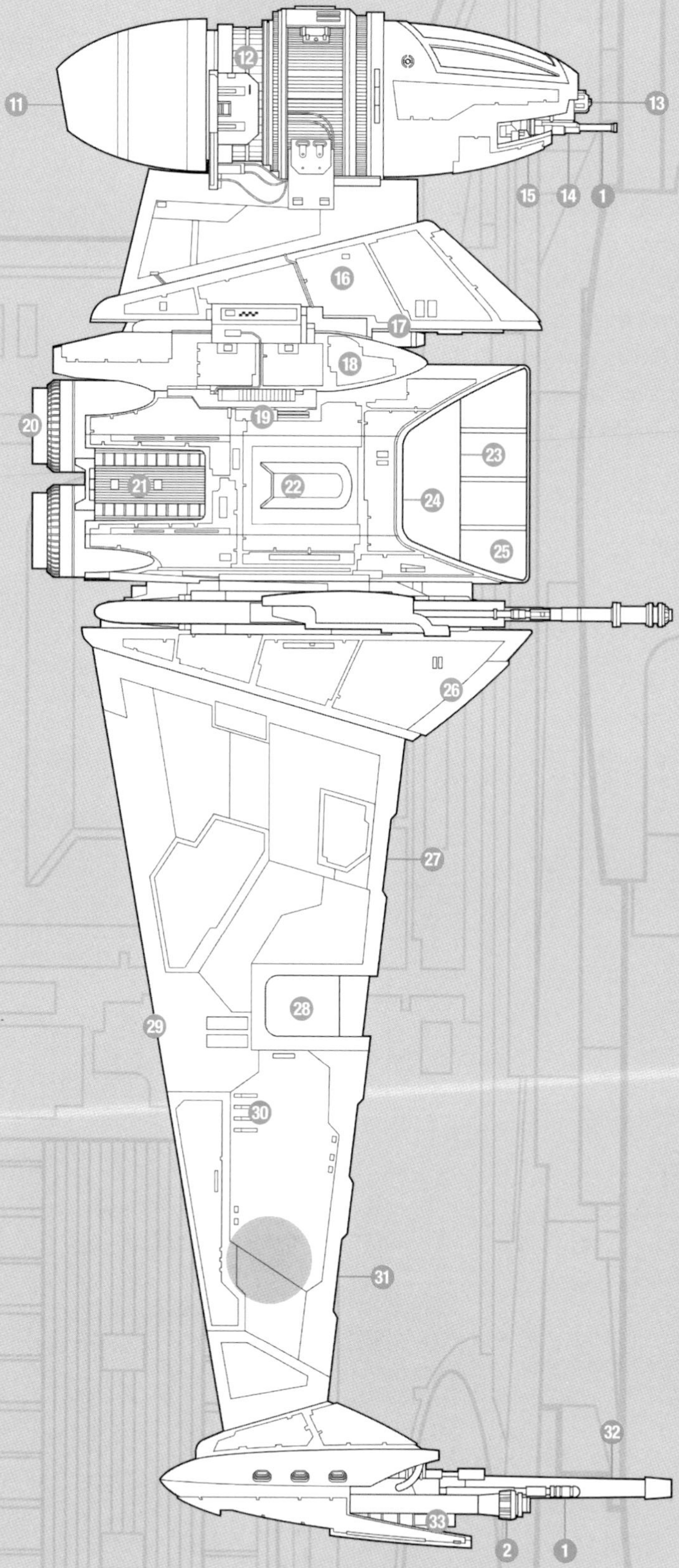

1. Low-power targeting laser
2. Ion cannon
3. Anti-gravity generator
4. Repulsorlift projectors
5. High-power energy cell
6. S-foil wing actuator system
7. Cockpit canopy
8. Long-range forward scanners
9. S-foil
10. Squadron markings
11. Escape pod sublight engine
12. Gyroscopic stabilizers
13. Short-range tactical sensor array
14. Twin auto-blasters
15. Weather radar
16. Deflector-shield generator
17. Secondary proton torpedo launcher
18. Deflector-shield projectors
19. Fusion reactor
20. Engine thrust nozzles
21. Hyperdrive
22. Reactor excess-plasma vent
23. Retro thrust nozzles
24. Main heat radiators
25. Cooling-system intake
26. Protective sensor-array window
27. Jammer system
28. Navigation sensor array
29. Primary wing
30. Wing status sensors
31. Velocity sensors
32. Heavy laser cannon
33. Primary proton torpedo launcher

◀ Slayn & Korpil designed the B-wing's unique weapon pod to hold the tightly configured ion cannon, proton torpedo launcher, and laser cannon.

A/SF-01 B-WING COCKPIT AND FLIGHT CONTROLS

The B-wing's automatic gyroscopically-stabilized command pod contained the starfighter's cockpit, life support system, flight computer, comlink transceiver, and sensors. When engaged, gyro-servos kept the pod in a fixed position, while the rest of the fighter spun, rolled, and twisted to evade defensive fire or "sweep" its weapons. Because the pilot remained stable within the cockpit while the rest of the craft rotated around the command pod, the pilot could concentrate on his or her flight path and targeting.

Slayn & Korpil engineers considered installing an astromech droid socket or integrated astromech into the B-wing before Quarrie, the creator of the B6 prototype, pointed out that incorporating droid technology would present expensive and possibly problematic technical challenges to the B-wing's electrical systems. Instead, engineers equipped the B-wing with a sensor-laden Microaxial LpM-549 navigation computer to make calculations necessary to navigate through hyperspace.

On the pilot's command, a unique fire-control and targeting computer could fire the laser cannon at very low power at a target. By firing continuously in this mode, the B-wing's targeting computer could gather enough data to provide near-perfect target range and vector information without inflicting damage on the target. Once the laser locked on the target, the ion cannons and/or proton torpedoes fired. Although the fire control-system ensured a 97% probability of hitting the designated target, it also revealed the B-wing's approach vector to the enemy. Consequently, B-wing pilots used the "low-power laser" targeting system sparingly, and many removed it entirely.

A/SF-01 B-WING CONTROLS

1. Multi-function display screen
2. Sensors
3. Navigation
4. System status
5. Safety
6. Weapons trigger
7. Control yoke
8. Power management
9. Engine status indicators
10. Weapons arming switches
11. Targeting scope
12. Circuit access panel
13. Air scrubbers

▶ Slayn & Korpil replicated and modified components from the B6 prototype's controls to create improved controls for the B-wing.

◀ When flying toward a target, pilots usually rotated the B-wing's cockpit "above" the primary wing.

▶ The Mon Calamari rebel pilot Ika Sulko's inherent kinesthetic sense aided his ability to operate within the B-wing's rotatable cockpit.

A/SF-01 B-WING WEAPONS AND DEFENSES

The B-wing provided much needed offensive power for the rebels on space combat missions. A triple battery of medium ion cannons, two proton torpedo launchers, a heavy laser cannon, and two auto-blaster cannons made the B-wing the most heavily-armed starfighter in the known galaxy. Most patrol craft and even some corvettes carried less raw firepower.

The B-wing's weapon pod held one of the fighter's three ArMek SW-7a ion cannons. The weapon pod also contained an emission-type Krupx MG9 proton torpedo launcher and a Gyrhil R-9X laser cannon. Between the port nacelle and the outer edge of the cooling system intake, an armored emplacement housed a secondary Krupx proton torpedo launcher. At the opposite end of the primary airfoil, the command pod's nose had a mount point that typically held twin Gyrhil 72 auto-blaster cannons; the mount point could accommodate other optional weapons, including an additional set of Gyrhil 72s for a total of four auto-blasters.

The ion cannons and proton torpedoes were linked to aim at the same target. Pilots could set the weapons to fire independently for maximum precision, together in salvos for maximum damage, or alternate for covering and interdiction fire. Although the B-wing had targeting systems that enabled weapons to fire automatically, pilots typically maintained direct control of the auto-blasters.

Slayn & Korpil also produced the B-wing Mark II. Decades after the fall of the Empire, Resistance technicians salvaged parts from the B-wing Mark II to refurbish engine pods from Republic-era shuttles.

▲ **At the Battle of Endor, the B-wing pilots of Blade Squadron took out the Imperial Star Destroyer *Devastator*.**

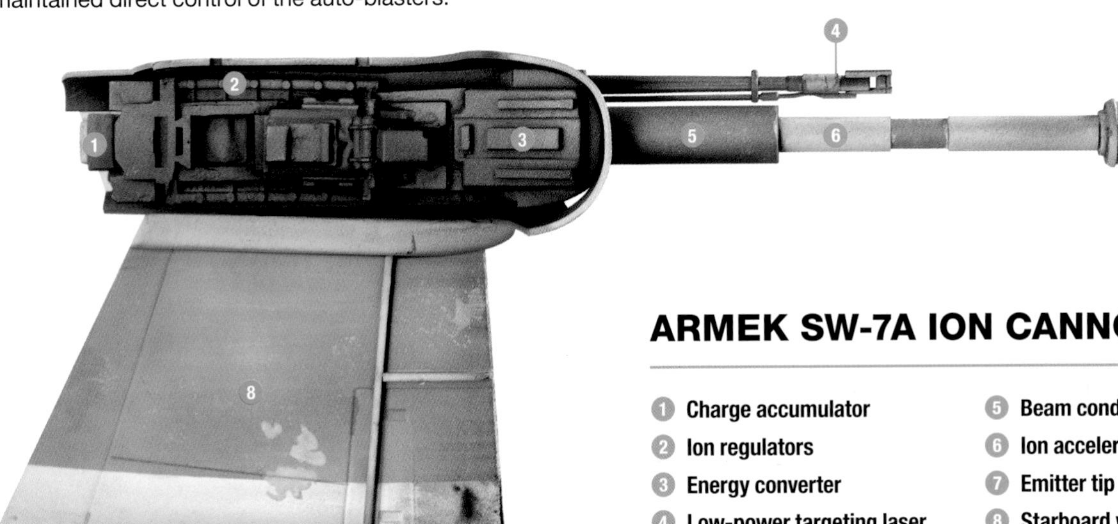

ARMEK SW-7A ION CANNON

1. **Charge accumulator**
2. **Ion regulators**
3. **Energy converter**
4. **Low-power targeting laser**
5. **Beam condensor**
6. **Ion accelerating barrel**
7. **Emitter tip**
8. **Starboard wing**

S-FOILS

1. Deployed configuration
2. Stowed configuration
3. S-foil wing actuator system
4. Ion cannon
5. Heavy laser cannon

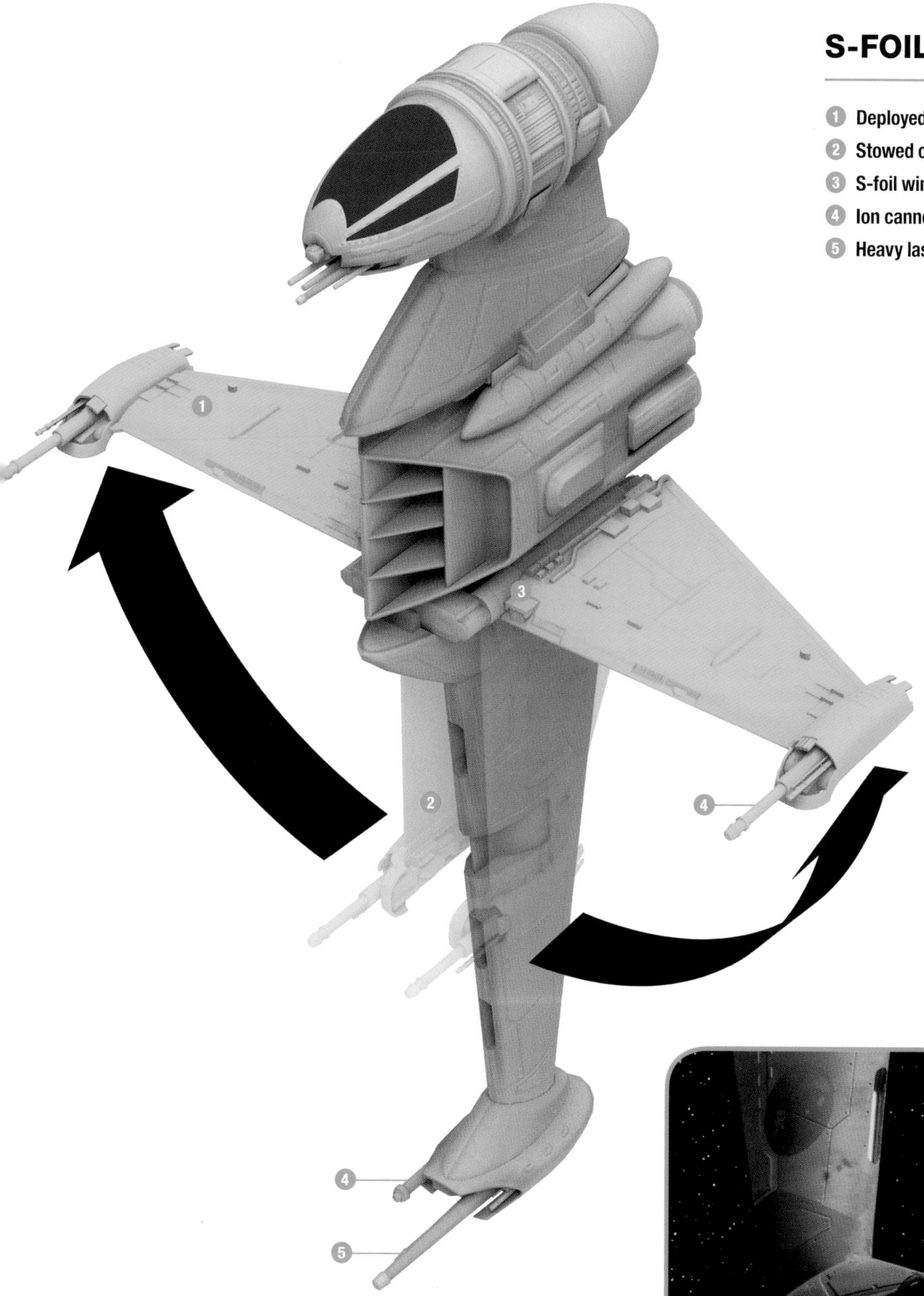

◀ Although similar in function to the X-wing's S-foils, the B-wing's S-foils incorporated more advanced actuator technology and magnetic locking mechanisms.

▶ The B-wing's SW-7A ion cannons were manufactured by ArMek, the company that also produced the SW-4 ion cannon for BTL-A4 Y-wing assault starfighter/bombers.

T-65B X-WING STARFIGHTER

After the fall of the Galactic Republic, the newly-formed Galactic Empire seized administrative control of numerous companies, including the starship manufacturer Incom Corporation, which had produced starfighters for the Republic Navy during the Clone Wars. Despite Incom's excellent reputation and the Empire's goals to create the largest fleet of warships in history, the Imperial Navy routinely disregarded Incom in favor of another manufacturer, Sienar Fleet Systems, which produced scores of inexpensive TIE fighters for the Navy.

When Naval officials announced that they wanted Incom to develop a new and more robust single-pilot Imperial starfighter, Incom had no choice but to comply. Incom engineers took design inspiration from two previous Clone Wars-era Incom starfighters: the short-range Z-95 Headhunter flown by the legendary Reaper Squadron, and the hyperdrive-equipped Aggressive ReConnaissance-170. Both fighters featured long, sensor-laden noses and wing-mounted laser cannons. The ARC-170 also featured moveable wings called S-foils, which opened to expose heat sinks and radiators to help cool the ship. Engineers incorporated aspects of both the Z-95 and ARC-170 into a prototype for the new fighter.

Navy officials approved the prototype, and Incom began production. However, the Imperial Bureau of Operations belatedly questioned and objected to the fact that each Incom starfighter cost more than twice the price of a standard Sienar TIE fighter. Soon, Imperial politics and corporate rivalries again sidelined Incom in favor of Sienar, leaving Incom with stagnant production and assembly facilities, and expensive unsold inventory.

When rebel cell agents met discreetly with Incom technicians and suppliers about obtaining starfighters, the sympathetic Incom representatives were more than eager to introduce the rebels to the fighter that the Imperials had ultimately dismissed: the X-wing.

— Excerpt from *Official History of the Rebel Movements*, Volume One

◀ The Incom X-wing starfighter was slower and less maneuverable than the standard Sienar Fleet Systems TIE fighter, but the X-wing's energy shielding and quad laser cannons gave rebel pilots a tremendous edge over their Imperial opponents.

X-WING ORIGINS

Prior to the Clone Wars, the starship manufacturers Incom Corporation and Subpro Corporation collaborated to produce the Z-95 Headhunter, a multi-purpose, single-pilot starfighter marketed to planetary defense forces. The Z-95 was originally equipped with two sublight engines and without a hyperdrive or astromech socket, but Incom/Subpro offered conversion kits to upgrade the Z-95 with a rudimentary hyperdrive and a navicomputer. Because even modified Z-95s lacked astromechs, pilots were required to pre-program hyperspace routes or use data chips to install jump coordinates into the navicomputer. Despite the Z-95's technical limitations, pilots appreciated its internal environmental controls, wingtip-mounted linked laser cannons, concussion missile launchers, and an optional proton cannon.

During the early stages of the Clone Wars, the Grand Army of the Republic commissioned Incom/Subpro to design a Z-95 Headhunter customized for the Republic Navy's clone pilots. The Navy utilized their Z-95s for both escort duty and starfighter combat. Like standard Z-95s, the clone Z-95 Headhunter lacked a hyperdrive but had more powerful shielding and weapons than standard versions. Incom/Subpro subsequently produced the larger, heavy-duty Aggressive ReConnaissance-170 starfighter, also know as the ARC-170, for the Republic Navy's clone pilots. The hyperdrive-equipped ARC-170 carried a pilot, co-pilot, tail gunner, and astromech droid, and the underside of the wings held two uncommonly large medium laser cannons.

Subpro eventually ended business operations, but the legacy of the Incom/Subpro venture lives on in Incom's X-wing starfighter.

▲ Customized specifically for clone pilots, the Republic Navy's clone Z-95 Headhunters boasted endurance and adaptability.

◀ Clone pilots referred to their Z-95 headhunters as "snubfighters," a term that others subsequently applied to various small starfighters.

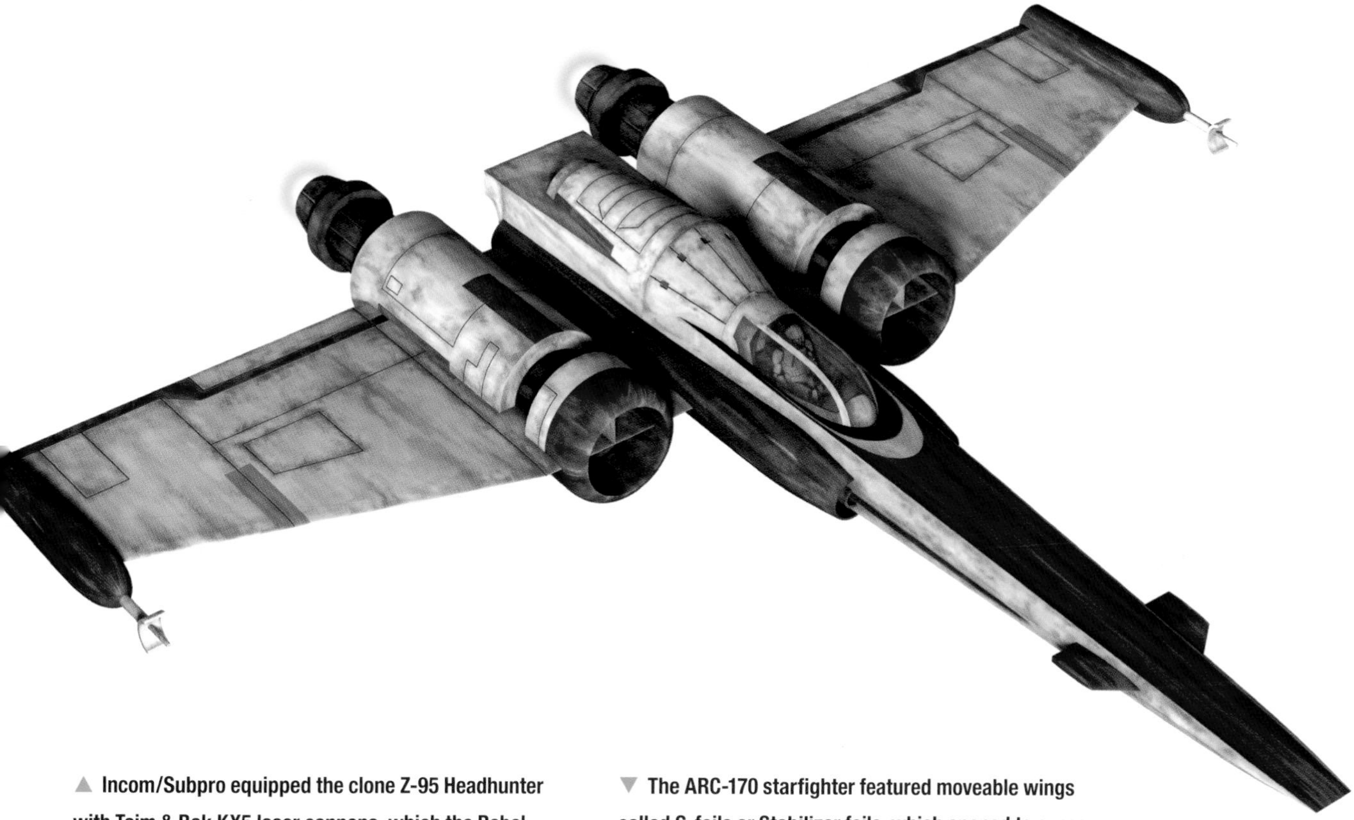

▲ Incom/Subpro equipped the clone Z-95 Headhunter with Taim & Bak KX5 laser cannons, which the Rebel Alliance sometimes used as an alternative to IX4 laser cannons on BTL-A4 Y-wing assault starfighter/bombers.

▼ The ARC-170 starfighter featured moveable wings called S-foils or Stabilizer foils, which opened to expose heat sinks and radiators to aid the fighter's shielding and thermal stability during battle or hot pursuit.

T-65B X-WING STARFIGHTER

Incom Corporation engineers dubbed their new starfighter the X-wing because of how the ship's double-layered, movable cannon-tipped wings formed an "X" when opened into attack mode, a configuration that increased the cannons' range of fire. In either wing configuration, the T-65B presented a small front and rear profile, and made a difficult target. Unlike most starfighters, the T-65B X-wing and subsequent X-wing models excelled at atmospheric flights, and were far more maneuverable than Imperial TIE fighters in atmospheres.

Rebel technicians attributed the X-wing's remarkable maneuverability to three factors. First, the differential thrust from the fighter's four Incom 4L4 fusial ion engines allowed the fighter to quickly adjust its trajectory. Second, each of the four retro-thrusters had high-mass electromagnetic gyros that helped swing the ship in tight curves. Third, precise bursts of retro-thrust fired forward through the turbine nozzles for increased control, an absolute necessity in combat.

The T-65B X-wing housed an armored cockpit module equipped with flight controls, a compact life-support system, and a Guidenhauser ejector seat. The pilot used a ladder or mobile access stand to climb into the cockpit before lowering and locking the armor-reinforced, photosensitive transparisteel canopy, which darkened automatically to shield the pilot from dangerous bursts or beams of light. An acceleration compensator helped isolate the pilot from deadly g-forces generated by high speed maneuvers.

In short order, the durable X-wing became the backbone of the Rebel Alliance Starfighter Corps, and a symbol of the rebellion against the Galactic Empire.

▲ Designed to excel in all areas of starfighter combat, the T-65B X-wing was highly maneuverable and heavily shielded. Because of the fighter's key role in victories against the Empire, the X-wing became a symbol of the Rebel Alliance.

◀ X-wing starfighters of Blue Squadron provide air support during a rebel assault on the Imperial security complex on the planet Scarif.

▶ Departing from a secret rebel outpost on Yavin 4, X-wing starfighters of Red Squadron race against time to attack the Imperial Death Star battle station.

SPECIFICATIONS T-65B X-WING STARFIGHTER

MANUFACTURER: Incom Corporation

AFFILIATION: Alliance to Restore the Republic, New Republic

MODEL: T-65B space superiority fighter

CLASS: Starfighter

LENGTH: 13.4 m (44 ft)

WIDTH: 11.76 m (38 ft 7 in)

HEIGHT: 2.4 m (8 ft 1 in)

MAXIMUM ACCELERATION: 3,700 G

MEGALIGHT PER HOUR: 100 MGLT

MAXIMUM SPEED (ATMOSPHERE): 1,050 kph (652 mph)

ENGINE: Incom 4L4 fusial thrust engines (4);

HYPERDRIVE: Class 1 Koensayr GBk-585 hyperdrive motivators (4)

SHIELDING: Chempat "Defender" deflector shield projector

NAVIGATION SYSTEM: Astromech droid

TARGETING SYSTEMS: Fabritech ANq 3.6 tracking computer; IN-344-B "Sightline" holographic imaging system

ARMAMENT: Taim & Bak KX9 laser cannons (4); Krupx MG7 proton torpedo launchers (2)

ESCAPE CRAFT: Ejector seat

CREW: Pilot (1)

LIFE SUPPORT: Equipped

CONSUMABLES: 1 week

COST: 150,000 credits new; 65,000 used

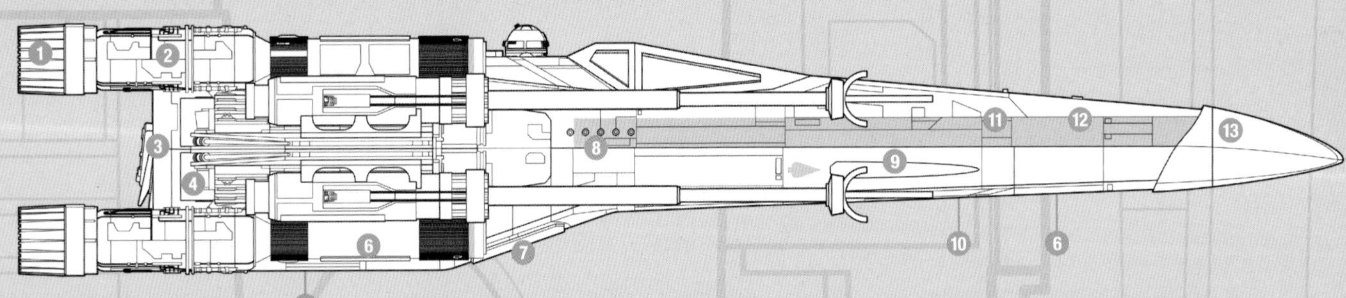

1. Exhaust nozzle
2. Fusial thrust engine
3. S-foil servo actuator
4. Fuel pump
5. Fuel tank
6. Landing gear door
7. Cargo bay door
8. Life support recharge ports
9. Torpedo launch tube
10. Repulsorlift
11. Subspace radio
12. Sensor computer
13. Primary sensor array
14. Squadron markings
15. Deflector ducts
16. Deflector shield projectors
17. Titanium alloy hull
18. Service cover
19. Hyperdrive
20. Deflector shield generator
21. Astromech droid socket
22. Cockpit canopy
23. Emergency canopy release charge
24. Flight computer
25. Sensor window
26. Nose cone
27. Engine access panels
28. Laser power line
29. Main cooling plates
30. Laser generator
31. Laser cooling sleeve
32. Magnetic flashback suppressors
33. Laser tip

Luke Skywalker and other rebel pilots typically used collapsible ladders to access the T-65B X-wing's cockpit.

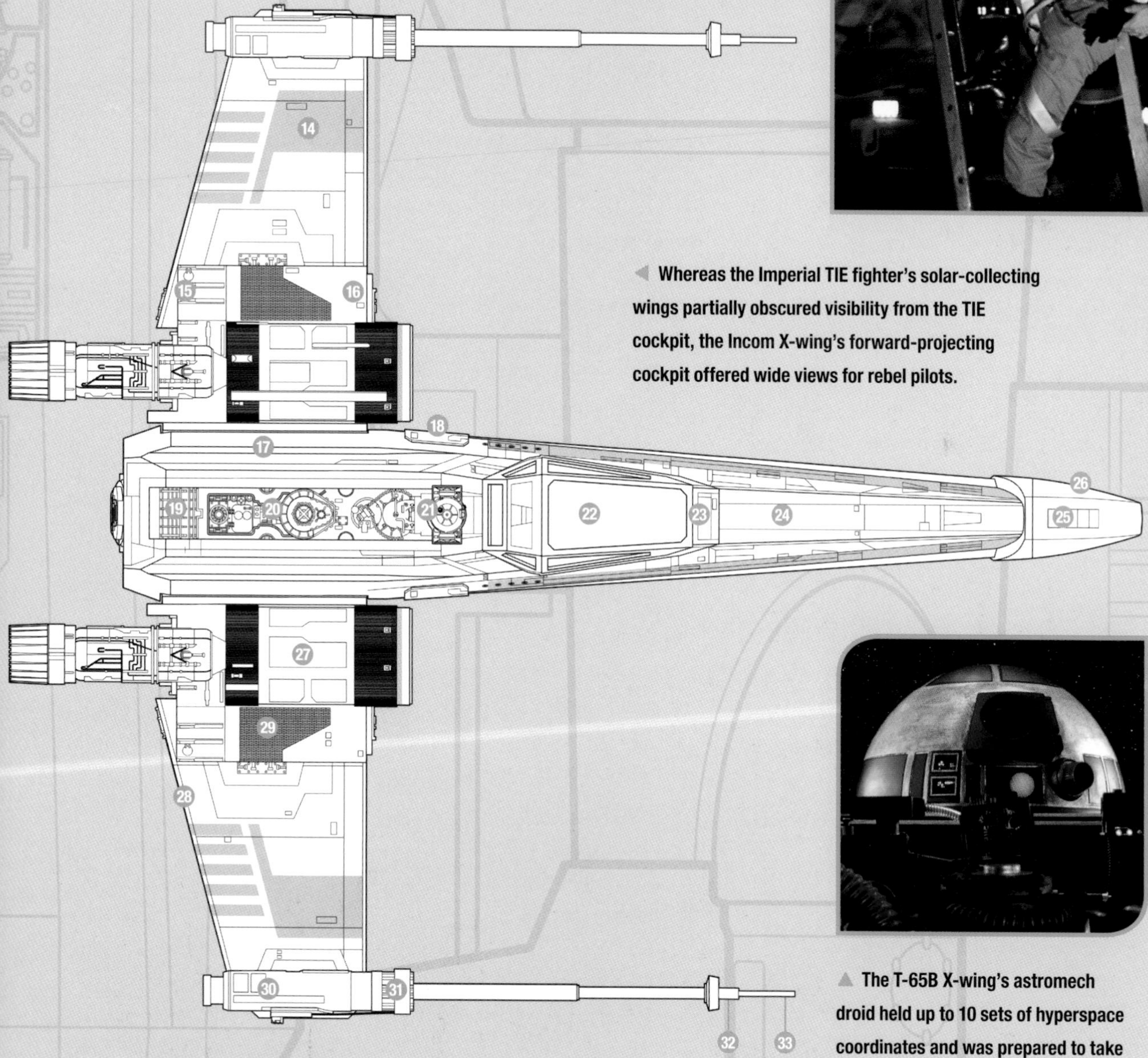

Whereas the Imperial TIE fighter's solar-collecting wings partially obscured visibility from the TIE cockpit, the Incom X-wing's forward-projecting cockpit offered wide views for rebel pilots.

14
15
16
17
18
19
20
21
22
23
24
25
26
27
28
29
30
31
32
33

The T-65B X-wing's astromech droid held up to 10 sets of hyperspace coordinates and was prepared to take full control of the starfighter—with or without the pilot in the cockpit—during emergencies.

VIEWS

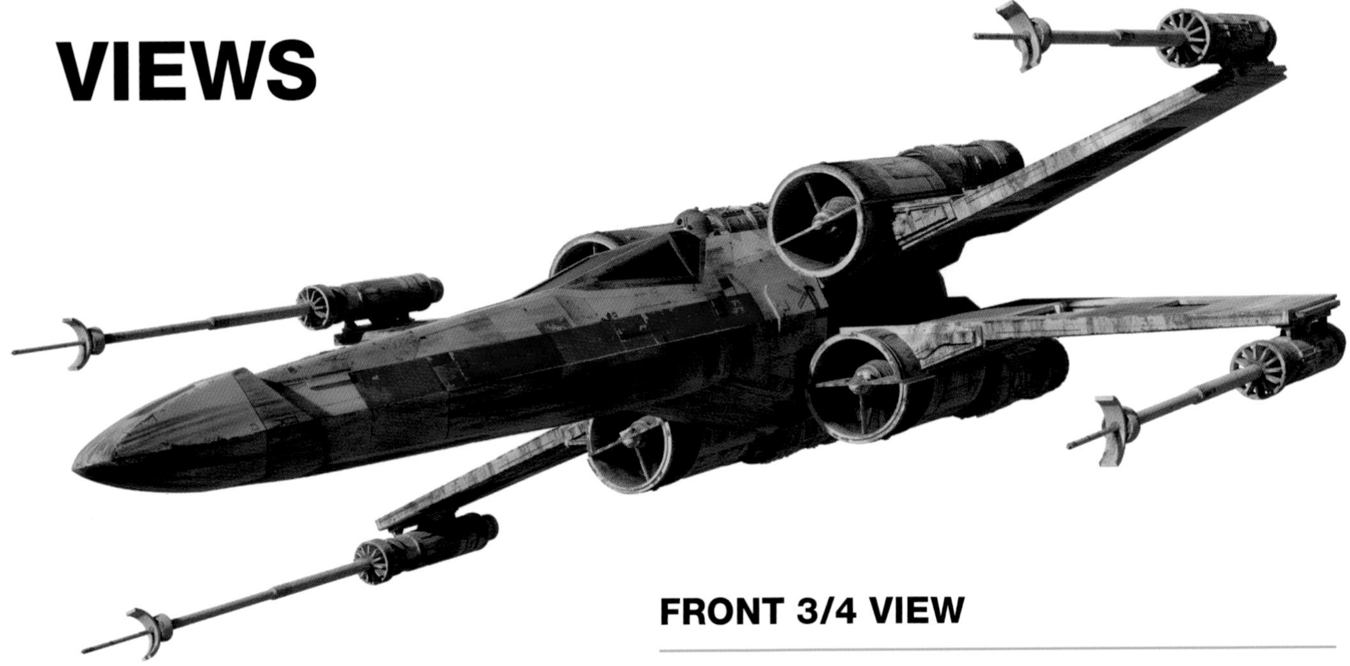

FRONT 3/4 VIEW

The front of the X-wing's long, narrow fuselage housed various sensor systems, including a Fabritech ANq 3.6 tracking computer, a Fabritech IN-344-B "Sightline" holographic imaging system, and a sensor array to locate and display tactical imagery on the pilot's targeting scope.

STARBOARD VIEW

Unlike Imperial starfighters, the X-wing was equipped for emergency bail outs. Separator charges blasted the cockpit canopy free, and a Guidenhauser ejection seat launched the pilot clear from the fighter. A separate ejector launched the X-wing's astromech unit from its socket.

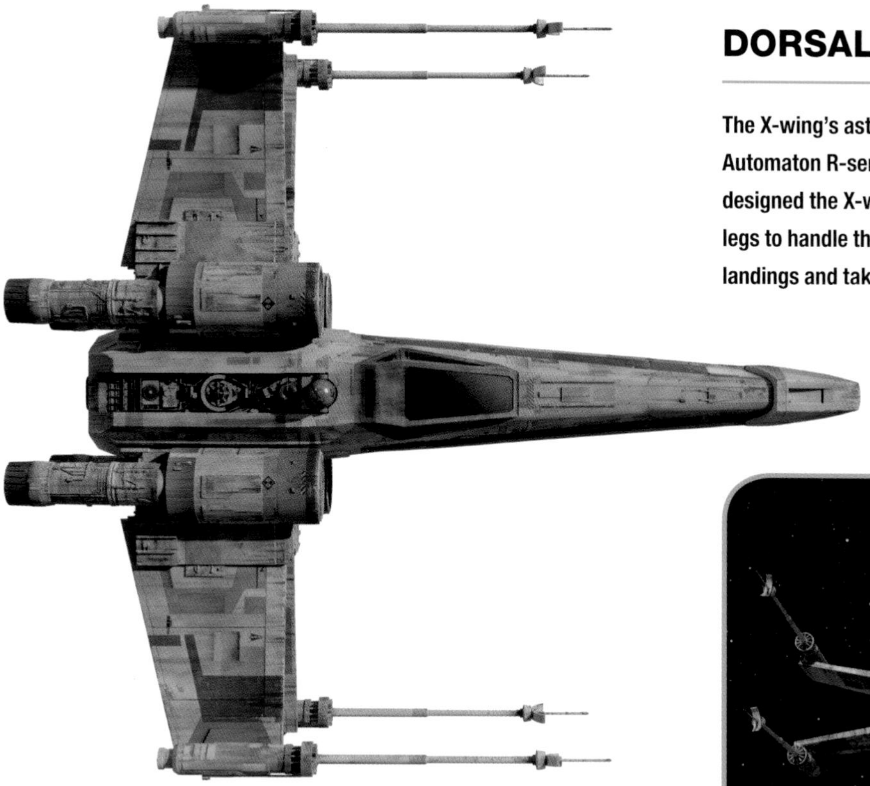

DORSAL AND VENTRAL VIEWS

The X-wing's astromech socket accommodated an Industrial Automaton R-series droid, typically an R2 or R5 unit. Incom designed the X-wing's three retractable, reinforced landing legs to handle the stress of operating the X-wing during rough landings and takeoffs.

FORWARD AND AFT VIEWS

Four massive Incom 4L4 fusial thrust engines flanked the X-wing's aft quarter, and propelled the fighter through realspace. A Fabritech k-blakan mini sensor scanned directly behind the fighter, and warned the pilot of approaching spacecraft and sensor sweeps.

T-65B X-WING STARFIGHTER S-FOILS

S-foils, also known as Strike foils or Stabilizer foils, are moveable wings that distribute deflector shield energy, and also serve as stabilizer surfaces in air travel. The difference between Strike foils and Stabilizer foils is that Strike foils carry weapons. Unlike Incom/Subpro's ARC-170 starfighter, which featured unarmed Stabilizer foils, the T-65B X-wing starfighter featured Strike foils with mounted laser cannons. Emplacements for deflector shield projectors were located along the leading edge of each S-foil, close to the sublight engines and fuselage.

Inside the S-foils, cryogenic capacitors—reserve power cells similar in design to the T-65B's primary power cells—stored additional power for the engines. The S-foils also contained enormous power couplings that enabled the power cells to share and balance energy reserves and output. An access panel at the rear of the T-65B-s fuselage led to the S-foil servo actuator, powerful twin servos that controlled all S-foil movement. Cold-weld arrestors locked the servos in position. In the event that the S-foil servo actuators malfunctioned or lost power, the T-65B's astromech droid could run diagnostics and attempt to make repairs or restore energy to the servos.

CRUISE MODE Rebel pilots kept their X-wing starfighters' Strike foils in the closed configuration as they traveled at sublight speed toward the Death Star battle.

ATTACK MODE With their Strike foils opened, Rebel pilots were ready to begin their attack on the Imperial battle station.

T-65B X-WING S-FOILS

1 Cruise mode
2 Attack mode
3 S-foil servo actuator
4 Power coupling
5 Weapon emplacement

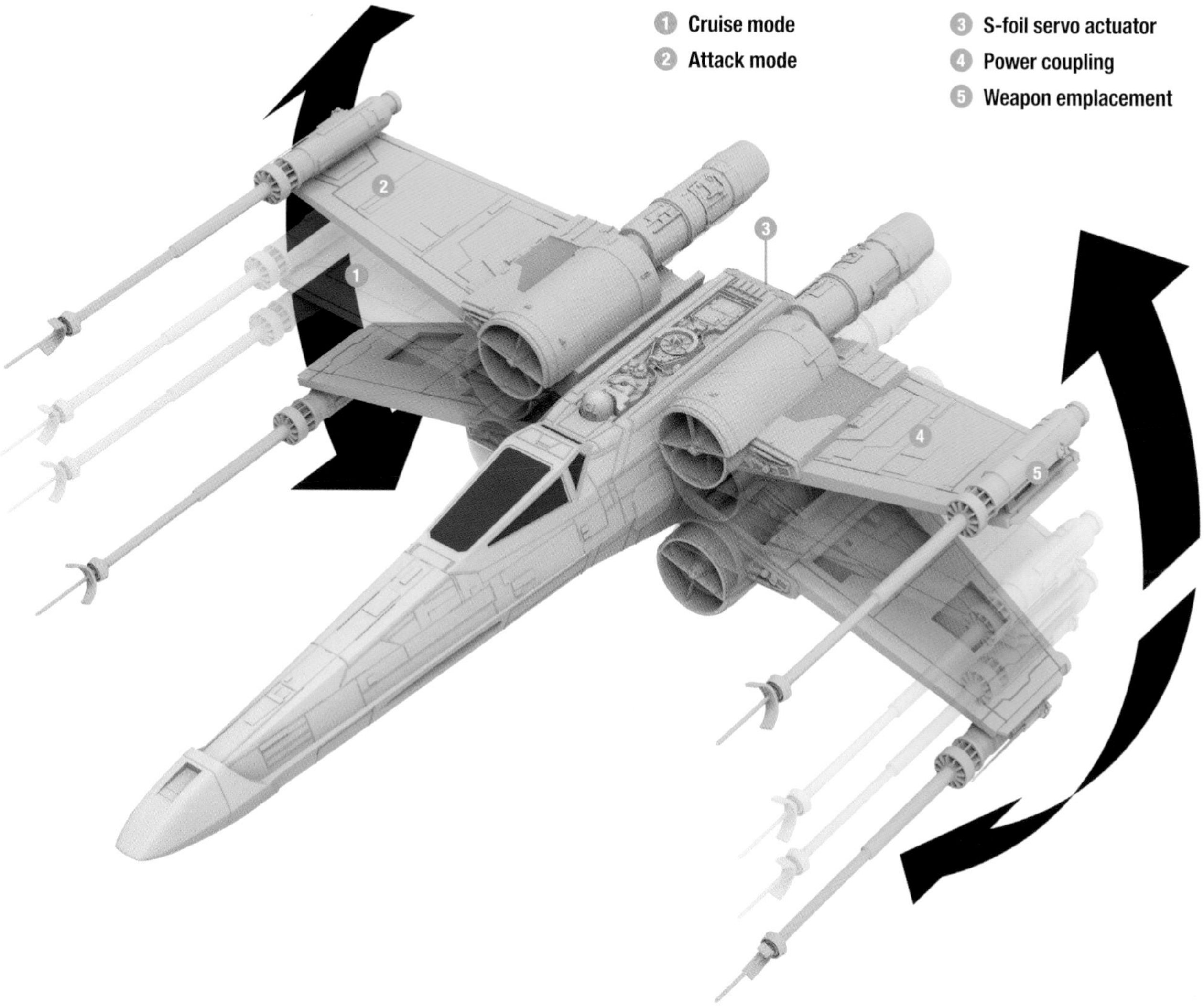

▶ When pilots set their X-wing's S-foils in attack mode, the deflector shield projectors mounted on the S-foils automatically expanded the fighters' protective energy fields.

T-65B X-WING STARFIGHTER SUBLIGHT ENGINES

Sublight engines, also known as sublight drives, move spacecraft through realspace. For the T-65B X-wing, Incom Corporation mounted an Incom 4L4 fusial thrust engine on each of the starfighter's four wings. On some T-65B X-wings, Incom alternately installed Incom 4j.4 fusial thrust engines, which were virtually identical to the more standard 4L4s.

Each fusial thrust engine contained durable high-performance, energy-efficient components. The T-65B's primary power cells—cryogenic cells located in the lower aft of the fuselage—stored the tremendous energy required to drive each engine. An Incom phi-inverted lateral stabilizer served to stabilize power flow into the engine, and a progressive combustion reaction power converter ignited and energized

▶ **Variable geometry exhaust nozzles regulated engine thrust for optimal performance. IR suppressors helped hide the hot exhausts from sensor detection.**

◀ **Centrifugal debris extractors prevent debris from entering the engine compartment, especially during atmospheric operations.**

T-65B X-WING SUBLIGHT ENGINES

1. **Cooling vanes**
2. **Centrifugal debris extractor**
3. **Electromagnetic gyros**
4. **Stabilizer**
5. **Power converter**
6. **Alluvial damper**
7. **Fission chamber**
8. **Turbo impeller**
9. **Turbo generator**
10. **Exhaust nozzle**
11. **Hyperdrive motivator**
12. **Power surge vent**
13. **Ground power input**
14. **Reactant agitator injector**
15. **Repulsorlift drive adaptor**

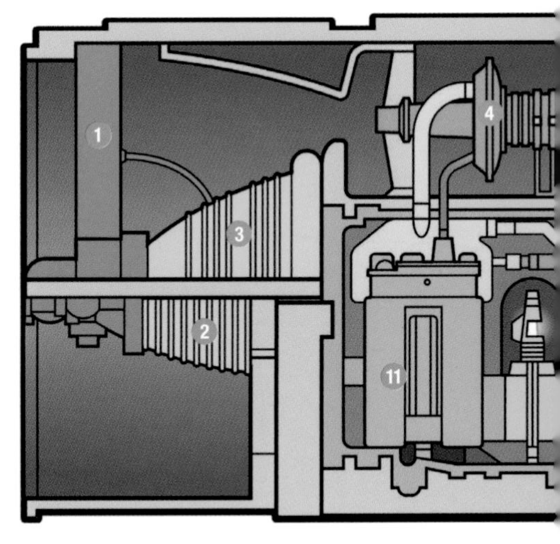

the engine with energy from the power cells. All four of the X-wing's converters energized the internal systems, deflector shields, and hyperdrive motivators in parallel.

Each engine had an alluvial damper, an internal servo-controlled absorption cone that controlled excess partial emission and fed into a fission chamber. Extremely volatile catalysts reacted through the fission with the convert output to produce tremendous thrust, the source of the engine's high sublight speed. Hot exhausts turned an inert first-stage turbo impeller to drive the turbo generator at slow speeds. When the power draw was low or the engine operated much above an idle, the turbo impellor locked into place. The impeller activated a turbo generator, which sustained itself at high engine speed and provided all circuit and electrical power to the engine. The turbo generators enabled each sublight engine to operate independently.

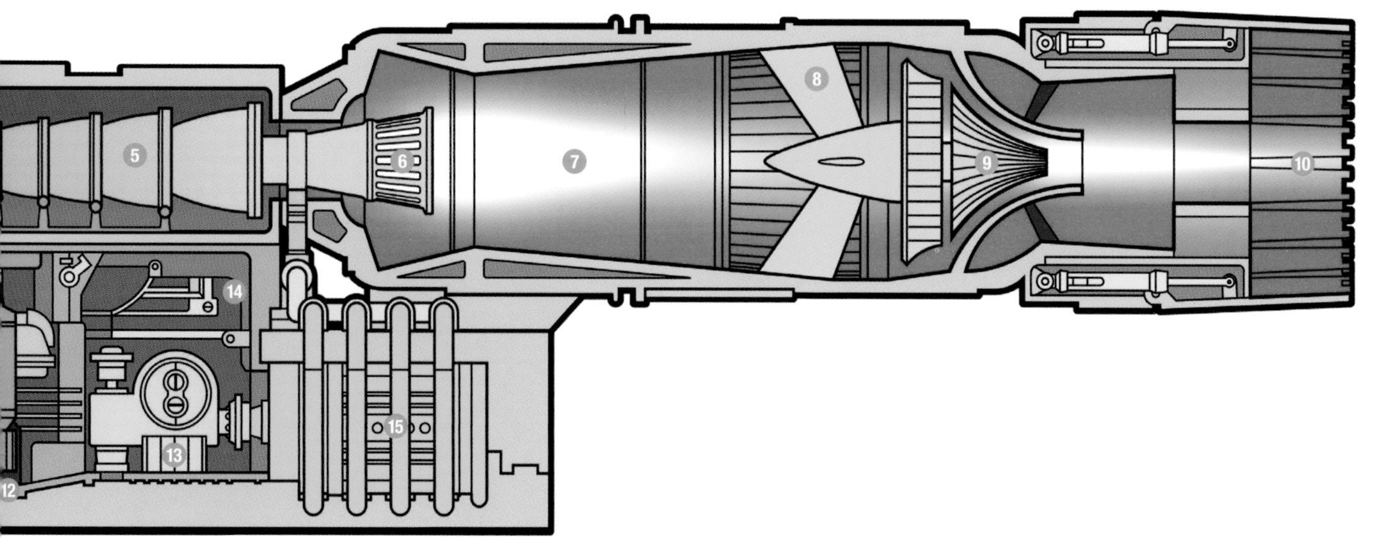

T-65B X-WING COCKPIT AND FLIGHT CONTROLS

The T-65B X-wing's armored cockpit module was equipped with a life-support system that featured compressors, a temperature regulator, and oxygen scrubbing filters, and could maintain a breathable, pressurized atmosphere for one week of non-combat operations. Incom designed the life-support system for human pilots, but rebel engineers could adapt the system for other species. Despite the proven safety of the life-support system, pilots routinely wore vac-suits as a precaution against hazardous decompression from emergency extravehicular activity.

Comprehensive displays allowed the pilot to monitor and control energy distribution throughout the X-wing. The primary display monitor was a multifunction instrument that pilots could pre-program for optimized readouts, streaming standard flight information with data related to tactical conditions, reconnaissance, and communications. The autopilot/astromech monitor provided data for the astromech's systems and served as a teletext translator, enabling the pilot to converse verbally with the astromech.

Like the BTL-4 Y-wing, the T-65B X-wing had an extendable targeting computer screen mask to assist the pilot with precise firing data during combat missions. The sensor array consisted of a Fabritech ANS-5d "lock track" full-spectrum transceiver, a Melihat "multi-imager" dedicated energy receptor, and a Tana Ire electrophoto receptor. A Fabritech k-blakan mini sensor provided the pilot with a view of the fighter's rear arc. The sensor array fed directly to the ANq 3.6 tracking computer, which could track up to 1,000 moving sublight objects, and acquire 20 possible targets; when programmed for extra sensitivity, the computer could track up to 120 specific sensor signatures.

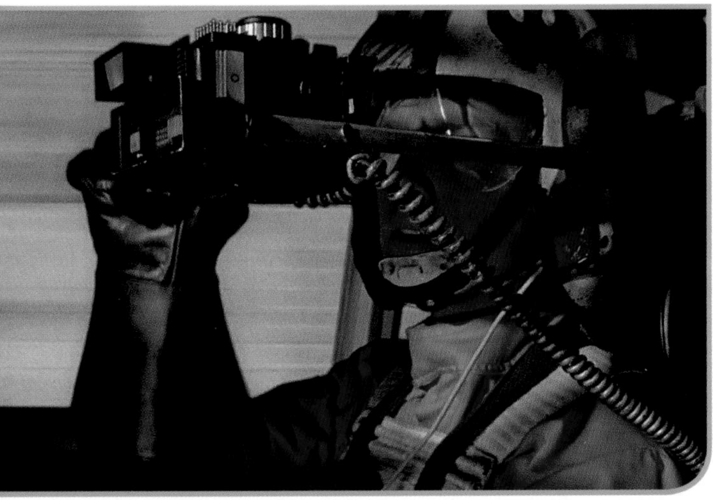

A targeting computer screen mask extended from a console located at the aft-port side of the X-wing cockpit.

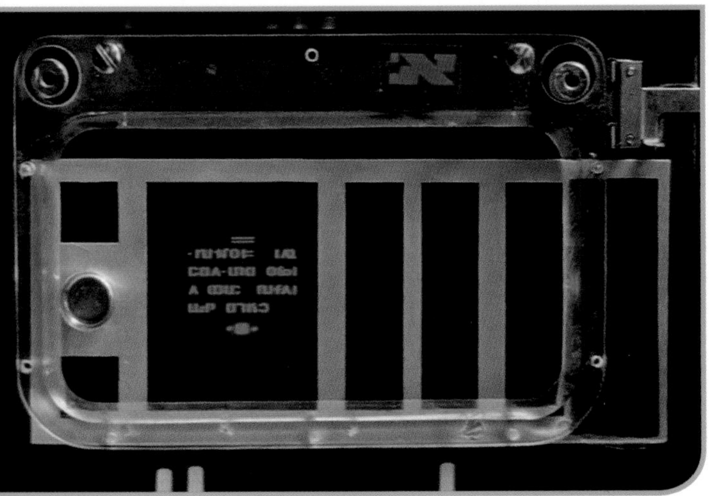

A droid-translator module in the X-wing's cockpit console enabled the pilot to communicate with the starfighter's astromech droid.

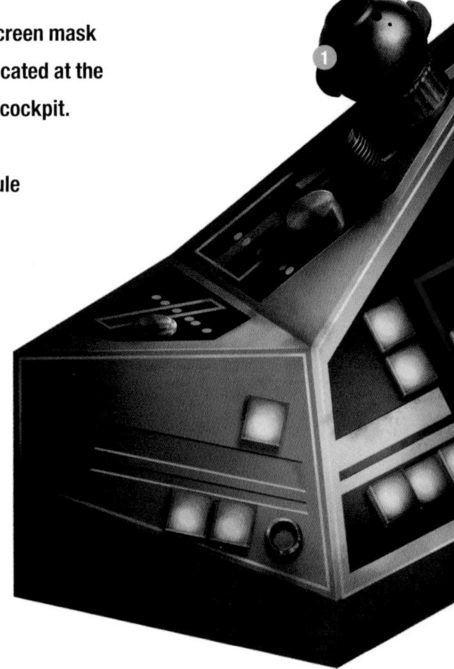

▶ The Incom T-65B X-wing's flight controls were similar to those on a popular Incom airspeeder, the T-16 skyhopper.

T-65B X-WING COCKPIT CONTROLS

1. Accelerometer
2. Altimeter
3. Attitude indicator
4. S-foil activator
5. Warning lights
6. Velocity indicator
7. Deflector shields
8. Communications
9. Primary display monitor
10. Targeting scope
11. Autopilot/astromech monitor
12. Computer indicator
13. Landing controls
14. Main system circuit breakers
15. Primary control systems interface
16. Fuel gauge
17. Chronometer
18. Inertial damper

T-65B X-WING WEAPONS AND DEFENSES

The standard T-65B X-wing's primary weapons were four forward-firing Taim & Bak KX9 laser cannons. Taim & Bak engineered the cannons' long barrels to provide a greater laser-firing range than other starfighters, but Rebel technicians modified the cannons to generate even more destructive power. Dynoric energy lines extended across the surface of the S-foils, and fed energy from the engine power converters to the lasers. When a pilot opened the X-wing's S-foils into attack position, the lasers targeted a specific "zero" point, typically 0.5 kilometer away. The pilot could set the cannons for single fire (each cannon fired individually), dual fire (starboard and port cannons fired alternately), or quad fire (all four cannons fired simultaneously).

For longer-range targets, the T-65B had two Krupx MG7 proton torpedo launchers housed in the main fuselage. Each launcher fired from a three-torpedo magazine for a total payload of six warheads. The T-65B was also equipped with a Bertriak "Screamer" sensor jammer that could block enemy starfighter sensors and thwart homing warheads.

In the aft section of the fighter, the X-wing's deflector shield generator produced basic shield matrices through a catalyzation process, and then fed deflector ducts scattered along the fighter's surface. The Chempat "Defender" projectors on the surface of the S-foils generated the starboard and port shields, and supplemented the X-wing's hardened titanium armor alloy hull.

▶ The T-65B X-wings' laser cannons were highly effective against enemy shield projectors and weapons emplacements as well as Imperial TIE starfighters.

▶ Taim & Bak utilized flow-control and optical compensation technologies to prevent the KX9 laser cannons' laser beams from scattering through atmospheres during supersonic flights, and to help the laser beams cut through atmospheres to the target.

TAIM & BAK KX9 LASER CANNON

1. Maintenance hatch
2. Static discharge coupling
3. Laser actuator
4. Primary beam generator
5. Coolant circulator
6. Coolant lines
7. Gas conversion enabler (XCiter)
8. Plasma combination injector
9. Prismatic crystal housing
10. Laser cooling sleeve
11. Laser blast condensing channel
12. Laser barrel
13. Gate coupling
14. Magnetic flashback suppressors
15. Laser tip

▶ Each KX9 laser cannon had a magnetic flashback suppressor that prevented overcharged or unstable blasts from damaging the cannon.

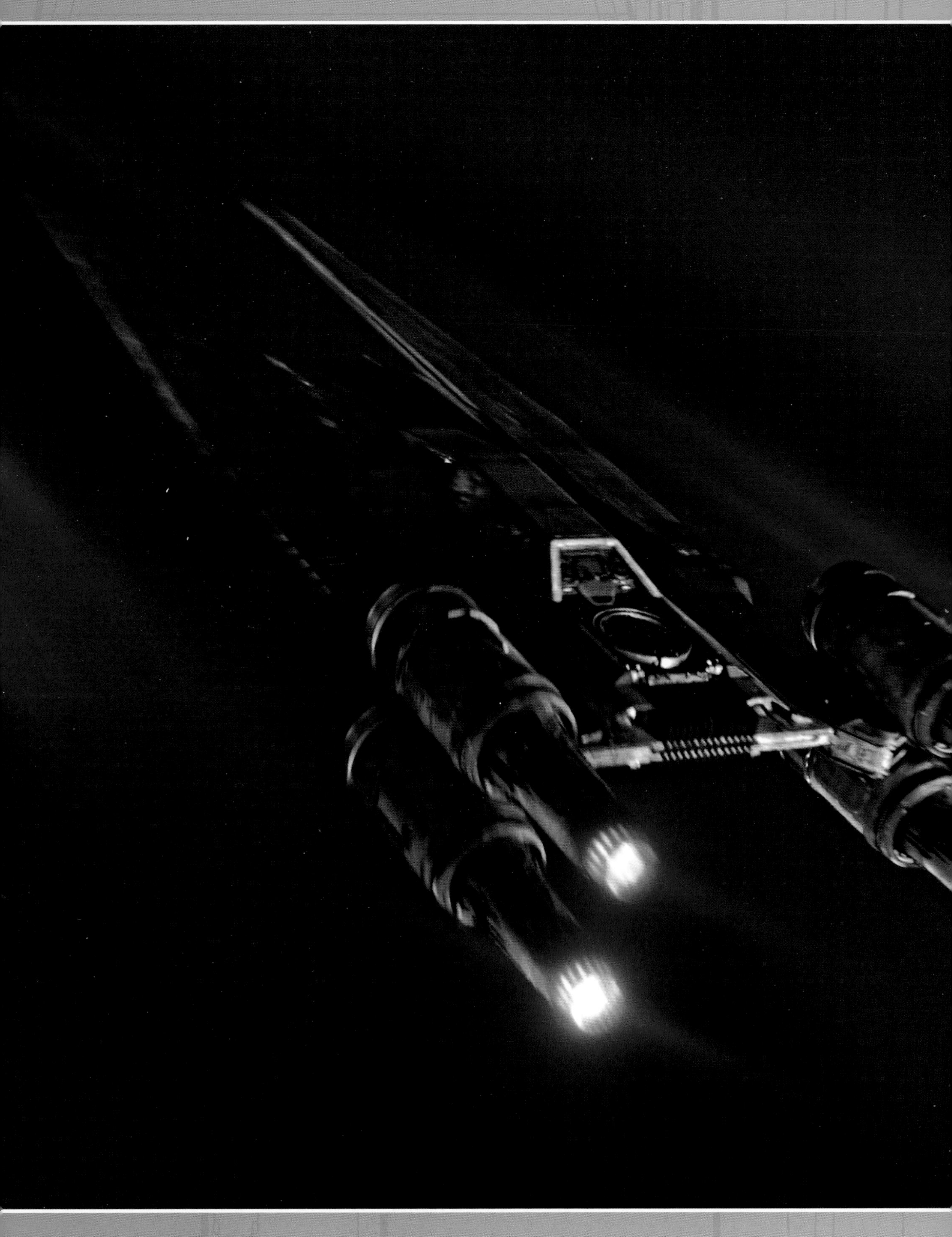

UT-60D U-WING STARFIGHTER

“We’re gathered here this morning because I wish to convey special information to you. This information is not from High Command. It comes straight from me. Straight from my heart.

I want you to know that I not only support you, but I admire you. And I hope you’ll forgive me if I struggle to explain why. But please keep in mind that I still consider myself a pilot more than a commanding officer. And I’m not one for speeches either.

Before I joined the Rebel Alliance, when I was the flight leader of the Rarified Air Cavalry of Virujansi, I became familiar with more than a few hotshot pilots. You know the type. I don’t doubt you even count them among your friends and allies, as do I. Because they not only get their job done, but they can be excellent company. Still, even the best of them... Sorry, like I said. Not one for speeches.

Oh, the hotshots. Too many enjoy basking in the glory of their skills, their daring maneuvers, and their kills. Over the past week, I have invested much of my time overseeing pilots training to fly X-wings. Like you, they come from all parts of the galaxy. Unlike you, they’ve demanded my attention in ways that I didn’t anticipate.

As U-wing pilots, you’re different. You’re not concerned with how many TIE fighters you shoot down, and how fast you shoot them down. Your concern, as you ferry infantry to and from battle zones, is keeping your passengers alive.

I say we let the hotshots have their moment. Because when I assigned you to fly U-wings, I didn’t choose you because you’re hotshots. I chose you because you’re better than that.”

—General Antoc Merrick, Commander of Rebel Alliance Starfighter Command and Blue Squadron, addressing Blue Wing U-wing pilots at Massassi Outpost

◀ Like the Incom T-65 X-wing, each of the Incom UT-60D U-wing’s four engines included a mounted GBk-585 hyperdrive motivator to initiate jumps into hyperspace.

UT-60D U-WING STARFIGHTER

The UT-60D U-wing starfighter was not Incom Corporation's first U-wing model, but it marked the end of an era for Incom, as the UT-60D was among the last designs that Incom released before the Empire nationalized the company. Due to timing and circumstances of the Empire's actions, Incom was unable to release a full production run of the UT-60D, which resulted in the craft's extremely limited availability. If Senator Bail Organa, a founding member of the Alliance to Restore the Republic, had not manipulated Galactic Senate records to make a rare shipment of UT-60Ds become "lost" while in transit to Coruscant, the U-wing might have never become part of the Alliance fleet.

The U-wing gets its name from its angular "U" shape, specifically when viewed from directly above or below. Incom conceived the UT-60D primarily as a transport for couriers or security forces, and intended to offer a range of customization options for the cabin, including a variety of passenger seats, convertible bunks, and a compact lavatory. The Empire forced Incom to scrap customization options for the UT-60D, but Incom salvaged various pre-planned options for their subsequently-produced civilian version of the craft, the BT-45D U-wing.

Incom did not design the UT-60D for dogfights or tight turns, a prerequisite for starfighters. However, both the Rebel Alliance Special Forces and the Starfighter Corps saw potential for the UT-60D as close air support for ground soldiers, and were quick to conscript the craft as a troop transport and gunship.

▼ **With brave rebel pilots behind the controls, U-wings penetrated heavy-fire zones to deposit soldiers onto battlefields and then fly air support during dangerous missions against the Empire.**

▼ Although Incom Corporation did not conceive the U-wing as a starfighter, Alliance technicians and mechanics transformed the vessel into a sturdy troop transport and gunship with minimal modifications.

▼ Because of limited availability, the Rebel Alliance had fewer UT-60D U-wings in their fleet than any other starfighter.

▶ The U-wing's moveable S-foils did not carry mounted laser cannons but served as stabilizers in atmospheric flights.

SPECIFICATIONS UT-60D U-WING STARFIGHTER

MANUFACTURER: Incom Corporation
AFFILIATION: Alliance to Restore the Republic, New Republic
MODEL: UT-60D U-wing starfighter/support craft
CLASS: Starfighter/gunship (after Alliance modifications)

LENGTH: 23.99 m (78 ft 8 in) with S-foils forward
WIDTH: 8.54 m (28 ft)
HEIGHT: 3.51 m (11 ft 6 in)
MAXIMUM ACCELERATION: 2,600 G
MEGALIGHT PER HOUR: 95 MGLT
MAXIMUM SPEED (ATMOSPHERE): 950 kph (590 mph)

ENGINE: Incom 4J.7 fusial thrust engines (4)
HYPERDRIVE: Class 1 Incom GBk-585 hyperdrive motivators (4)
SHIELDING: Chempat deflector shield generator
NAVIGATION SYSTEM: Microaxial HyD modular navicomputer
TARGETING SYSTEMS: Fabritech ANq 2.9 tracking computer; IN-344-B "Sightline" holographic imaging system

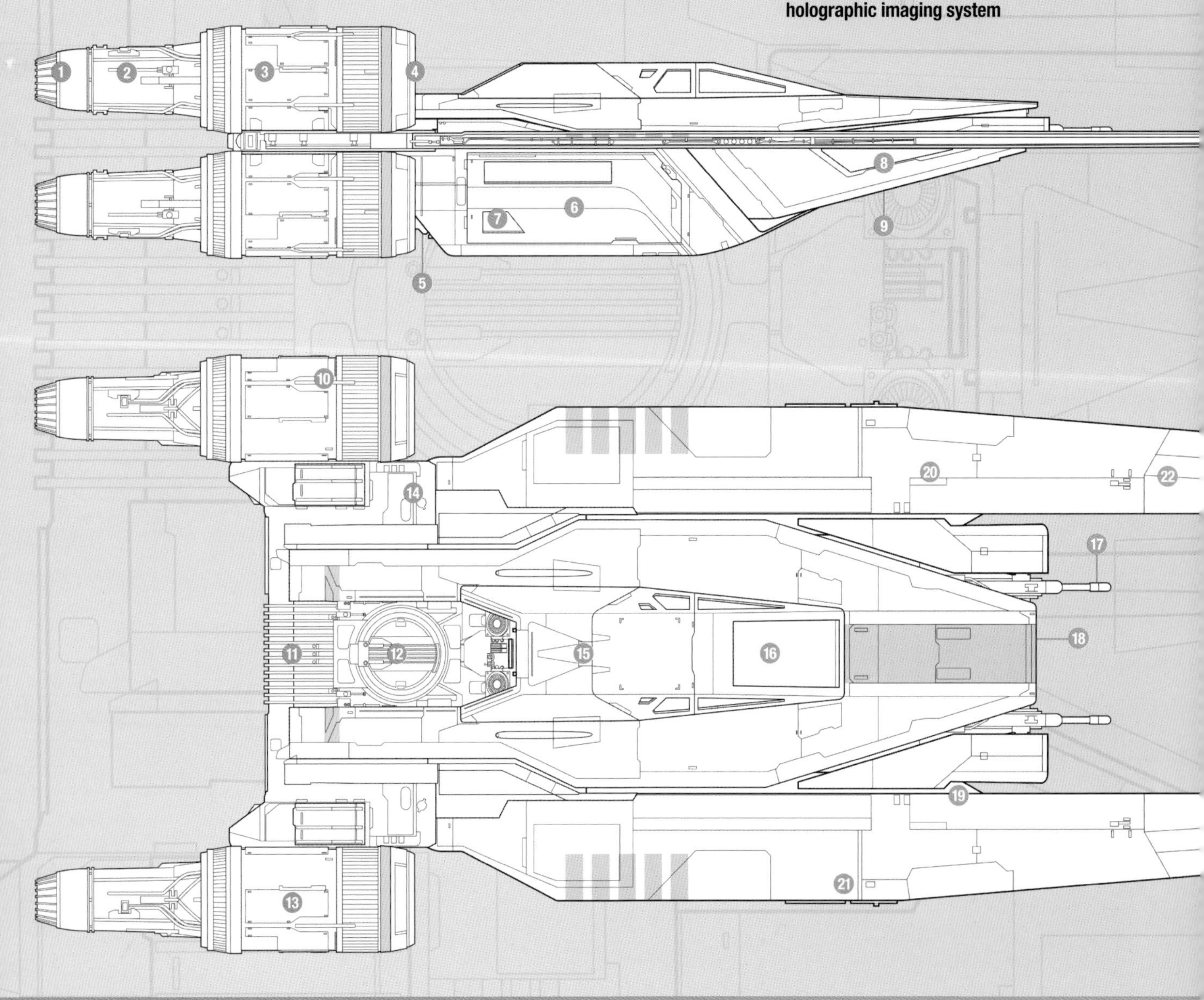

ARMAMENT: Taim & Bak KX7 laser cannons (2); Infantry-based heavy weapons (up to 2, optional)
ESCAPE CRAFT: Ejector seats
CREW: Pilots (2); door gunners (up to 2, optional)
LIFE SUPPORT: Equipped
CONSUMABLES: Two weeks
COST: 65,000 credits

▲ The Rebel Alliance's commitment to use the U-wing as close air support for ground soldiers bonded the operational divisions of the Alliance Special Forces (SpecForces) and the Starfighter Corps, two groups that otherwise had very little interface in military operations.

◄ The same design team responsible for the Incom Corporation T-47 airspeeder created the U-wing starfighter's wedge-shaped cabin.

23 24

1. Exhaust nozzles
2. Fusial thrust engines
3. Hyperdrive motivator
4. Energy intake cooling vanes
5. Repulsorlift field generator
6. Sliding main entry door
7. Emergency door release
8. Reinforced lower viewport
9. Ventral cockpit viewport
10. Engine cooling vents
11. Radiator/repulsor block cooling fins
12. Reactor power plant
13. Engine access panels
14. S-foil articulation servomotor assembly
15. Cabin interior
16. Dorsal cockpit viewport
17. Laser cannons
18. Primary sensor array
19. Wing catch bracket
20. Deflector shield generator
21. Deflector shield radiating plane
22. Integral subspace antenna array
23. Conductive mesh for shield energy distribution
24. Cryogenic power cells

VIEWS

FRONT 3/4 VIEW

The U-wing was equipped with a hyperdrive, but the Rebel Alliance discouraged using the vessel for long-range operations because life-support requirements for the crew would greatly increase fuel demands beyond efficiency.

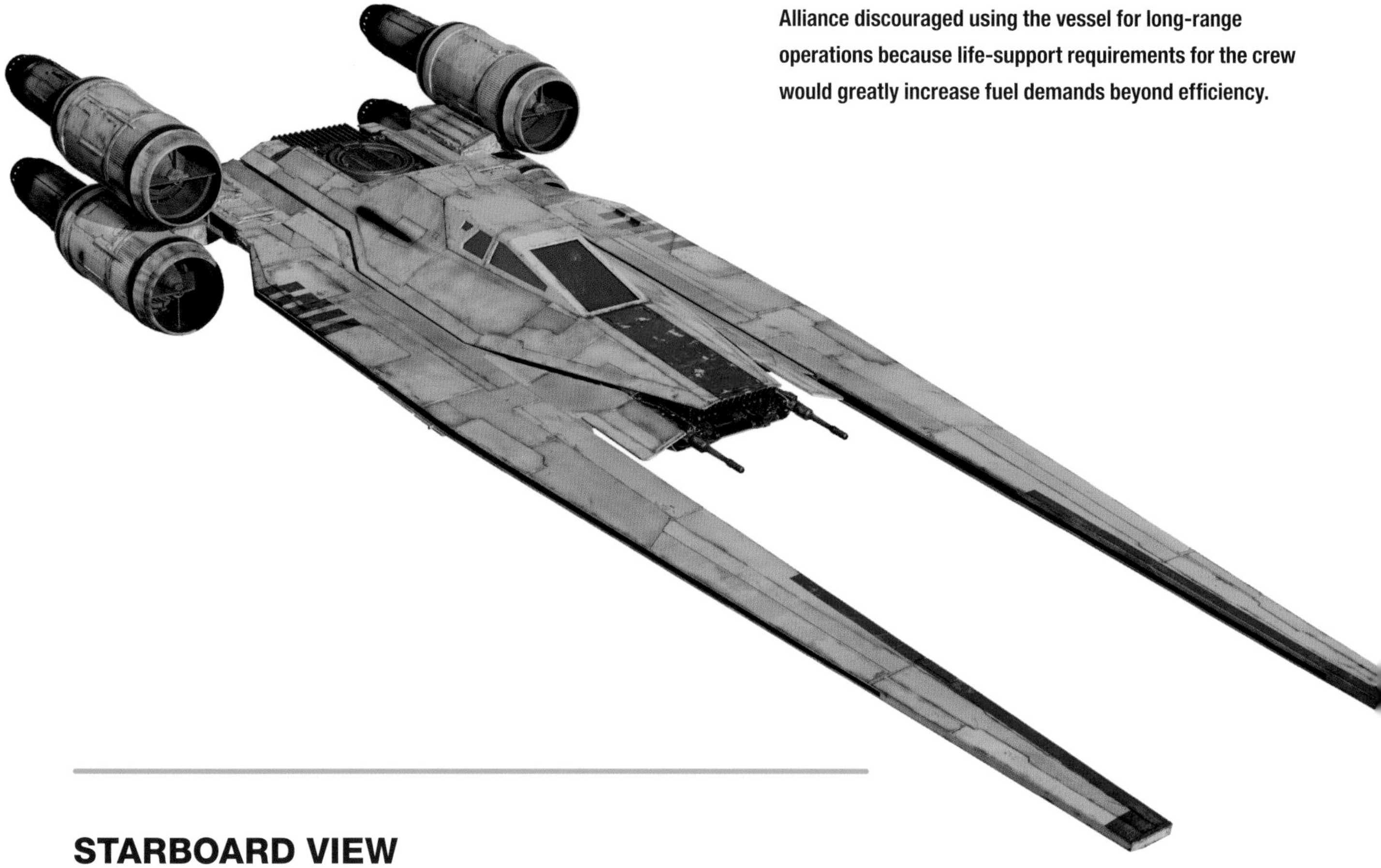

STARBOARD VIEW

The Rebel Alliance used the U-wing's large sliding doors for deploying and recovering troops, and also as stations for gunners.

DORSAL AND VENTRAL VIEWS

Although equipped with standard starship sensors to assist pilots during take-offs and landings, the U-wing's ventral transparisteel viewports allowed pilots to see objects directly beneath the craft, an invaluable asset when deploying or recovering troops during combat missions.

FORWARD AND AFT VIEWS

Incom engineers took inspiration from the engine configuration on their own T-65B X-wing fighter when they installed fusial thrust engines above and below the S-foils on each side of the U-wing's fuselage.

UT-60D U-WING STARFIGHTER S-FOILS

Incom's older U-wing models featured two long, rigid wings that extended forward on either side of the fuselage, and two large fusial thrust engines located at the aft. For the UT-60D, Incom's innovations included replacing the rigid wings with S-foils to create a swing-wing vessel, and installing additional engines above the existing pair for a total of four engines. By adjusting the positions of the S-foils, pilots could increase or redirect coverage from the craft's energy shields, and also increase maneuverability while flying through atmospheres.

UT-60D S-FOILS

1. Stowed configuration
2. Wing catch bracket
3. S-foil articulation servomotor assembly
4. Deployed configuration

▶ **Because the U-wing's S-foils extended into the pilots' visual range when angled forward, pilots could effectively increase visibility simply by shifting the U-wing's S-foils to the swept-back deployed configuration during atmospheric flights.**

▶ **At the U-wing's fore, mounted along the outer edges of the fuselage, port and starboard wing-catch brackets secure the S-foils in stowed configuration.**

▶ **In defense configuration, the U-wing's S-foils increased the deflector shield spread around the entire vessel.**

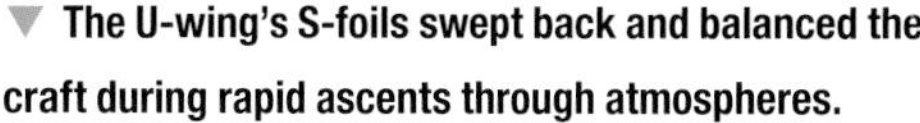

▶ **The U-wing's reactor powered the S-foil servomotors as well as the four fusial thrust engines.**

During flights through atmospheres, pilots adjusted the U-wing's S-foils to swing outward and back, which increased the craft's wingspan as well as maneuverability. Because atmospheric conditions could make wing deployment difficult, pilots usually reserved the outstretched configuration for high-altitudes. The shielding and armor of a U-wing adds to an operational mass on top of a hold full of passengers. In short, a U-wing handles much more like a heavy repulsorcaft than a swift space-superiority vessel.

▼ **The U-wing's S-foils swept back and balanced the craft during rapid ascents through atmospheres.**

▼ **U-wing pilots typically kept the U-wing's S-foils in deployed configuration until the craft entered space.**

UT-60D U-WING COCKPIT AND FLIGHT CONTROLS

Unlike most starfighters, the UT-60D U-wing's cockpit had two side-by-side, front-facing seats for a pilot and copilot, tandem controls, and ventral viewports; behind the cockpit, a cabin accommodated eight passengers. As nearly all other rebel starfighters were built for a single pilot, and because the Alliance often pressed any available equipment into applications that were never imagined by starship designers, the rebels used their small number of U-wings as troop transports, gunships, medevac lifters, courier ships, and shuttles.

A single pilot could operate the craft, but a flight team of two could better handle landing zone fire suppression and defense. The UT-60D featured standardized Incom controls that were similar to controls for Incom-manufactured civilian aircraft, an aspect that enabled pilots to smoothly transition from aircraft to spacecraft. Incom also produced the BT-45D U-wing, a civilian version of the craft with similar flight controls. Stripped of all its military offensive and defensive applications, and lacking a hyperdrive, the BT-45D found favor with private security forces on a few scattered worlds in the Mid Rim.

▼ **The U-wing's utilitarian cabin made long journeys across hyperspace impractical for more than several passengers.**

U-WING FLIGHT CONTROLS

1. Power levels
2. Threat indicator screen
3. Weapons trigger
4. Control handle
5. Weapons arming switches
6. Primary display monitor
7. Target designator reticle
8. System menu selector

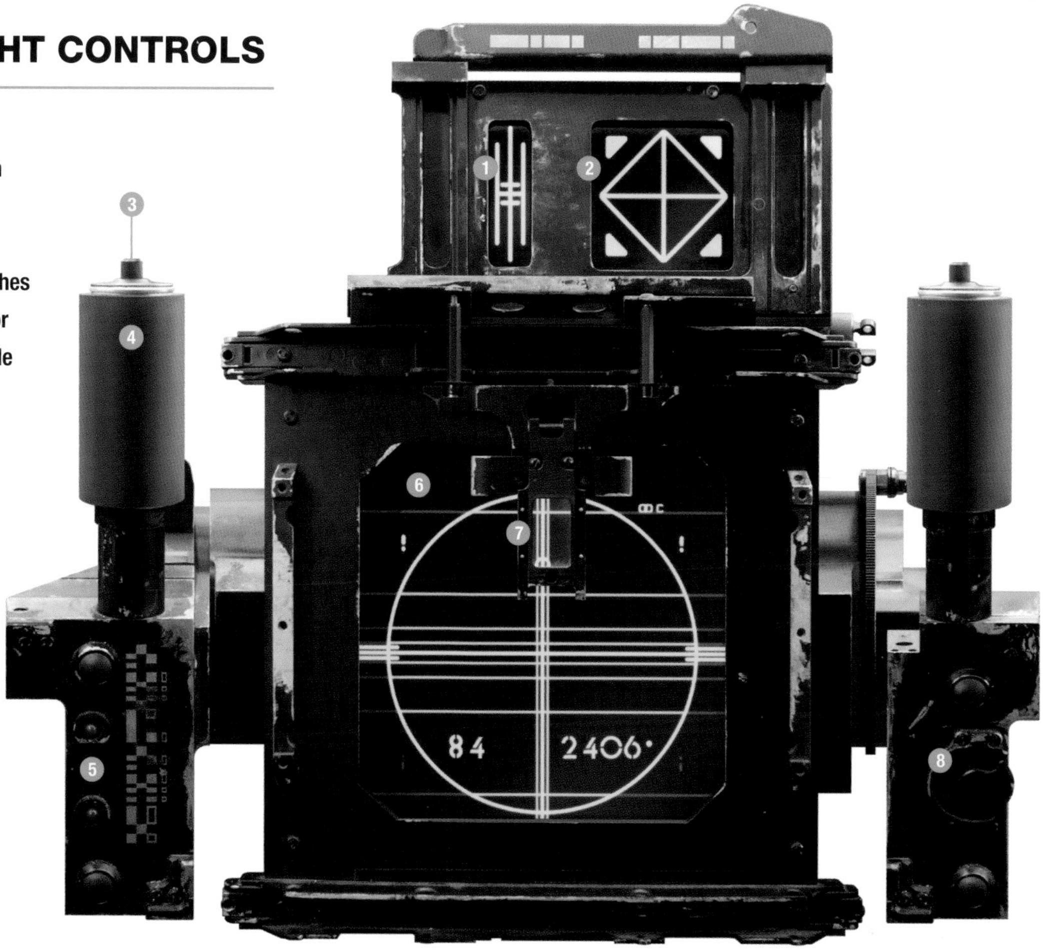

▶ The U-wing's side-by-side controls held central monitors that displayed flight, power, navigational, and targeting data to the pilot and copilot.

▶ The control to activate the U-wing's hyperdrive was centrally located on a console above the pilots' seats.

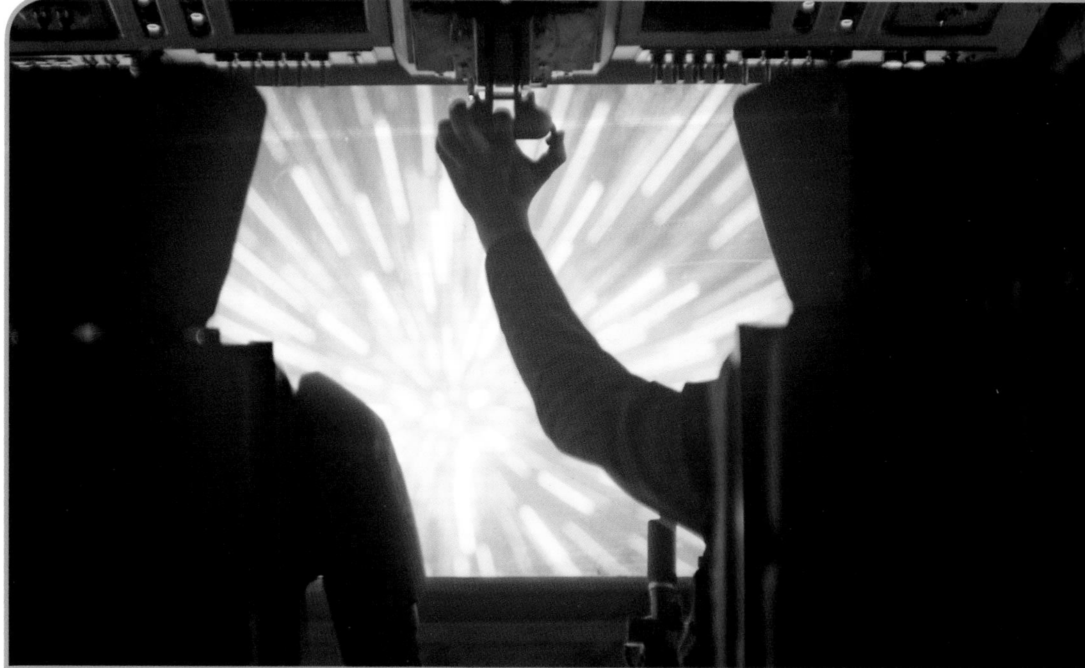

UT-60D U-WING WEAPONS AND DEFENSES

The U-wing's primary weapons were two fixed-position Taim & Bak KX7 laser cannons. Because the cannons were not maneuverable, pilots could only fire at targets directly in front of them, which limited the U-wing's application in ground support. Instead of refitting the U-wing with maneuverable cannons or side-firing modifications, rebel engineers installed improvised weapon mounts to transform one or both of the loading doors into gunports. Thus, rebel soldiers could utilize any infantry-based heavy weapon as part of the U-wing's arsenal, and effectively transform the starfighter into a gunship.

Although rebel door-gunners had numerous options for blaster weapons, records indicate gunners favored the BlasTech "Roba" M-45 repeating ion blaster for shooting enemy vehicles and vessels. A rapid-fire and traditionally hand-held firearm, the M-45 was easily fitted onto a stabilized pintle mount, and fired powerful blasts of ionized energy that could disable the electrical systems of targeted machinery.

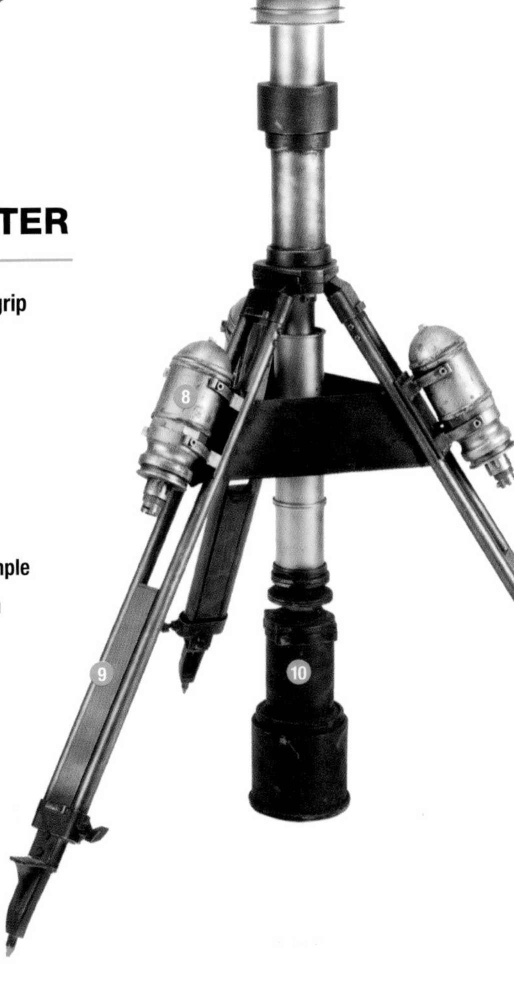

"ROBA" M-45 REPEATING ION BLASTER

1. Ventilated ion accelerating barrel
2. Barrel brace
3. Ion regulators
4. Electromagnetic sight
5. Power charge system
6. Magnatomic adhesion grip
7. Shoulder stock
8. Recoil compensators
9. Tripod stabilizers
10. Mounting post

◀ Broad side doors provide ample room for weapon emplacements.

▲◥ Alliance Corporal Bistan, a native of Iakar, manned a "Roba" M-45 repeating ion blaster when he served as the door gunner of a Blue Squadron U-wing at the Battle of Scarif.

▼ Taim & Bak manufactured the U-wing's KX7 laser cannons. The Galactic Empire used the same model cannons for some Imperial ships, notably the *Zeta*-class cargo shuttle.

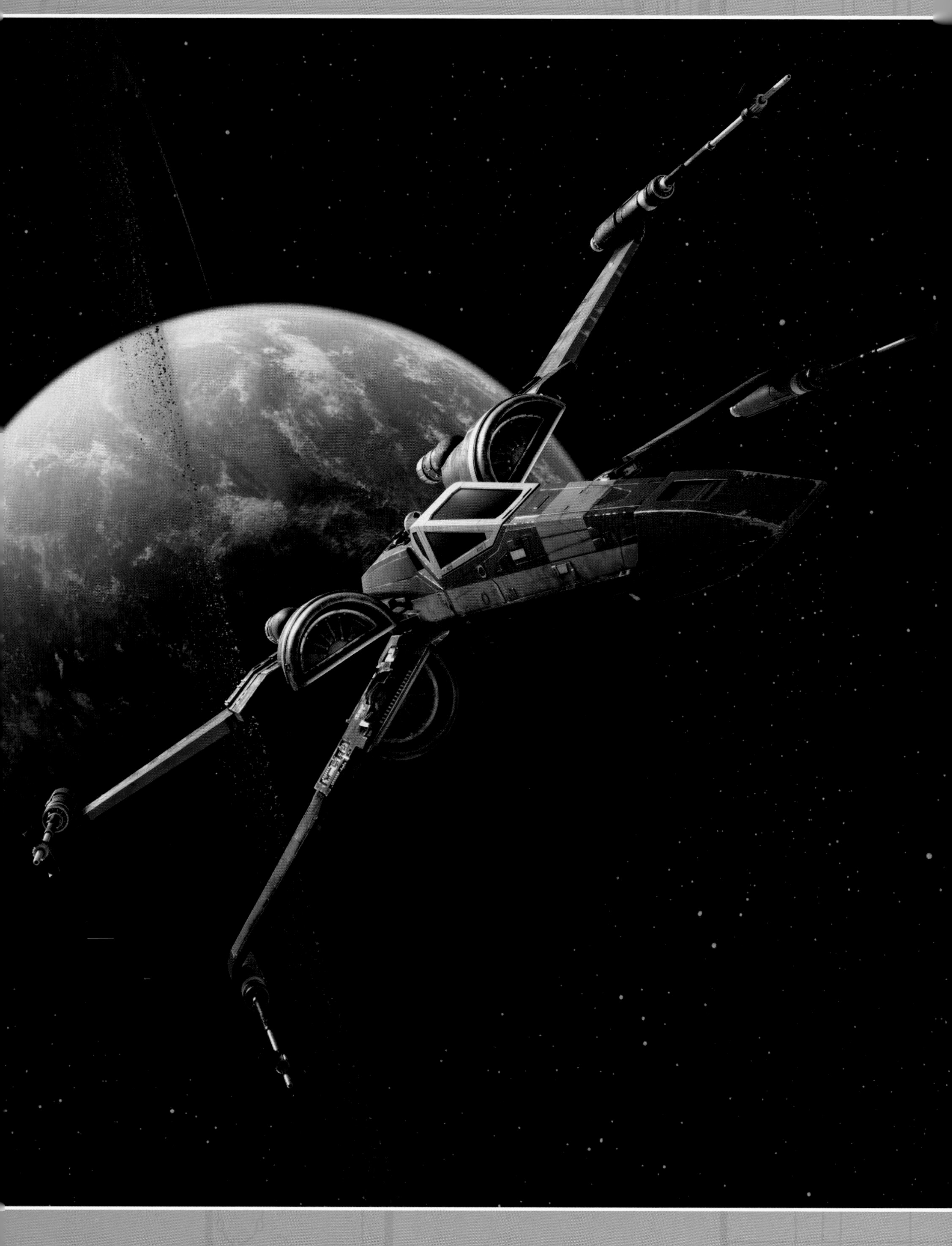

RESISTANCE STARFIGHTERS

Classified Communique
To: Resistance High Command
From: General Leia Organa

As you know, the Senate maintains that the First Order does not pose a threat to the New Republic. But reports from our own Resistance agents tell a different story, that the First Order has taken great measures to maintain secrecy of their organization and activities, and that they've been making rearmament efforts in violation of the Galactic Concordance. Given that all reports indicate renegade Imperial hard-liners founded the First Order, and also that Sienar-Jaemus Fleet Systems has been constructing vessels for the First Order, we can be certain that the First Order is building a fleet. At this time, we can only guess the size of the First Order's fleet.

I wish I could say we've been down this path before, that our situation is no different than when the Rebel Alliance sought support from others who opposed the Empire. But this situation is not the same. Whatever the rebellion accomplished at the Battle of Endor, we must consider that the fall of the Empire led directly to the rise of the First Order, and that the First Order could be far more ruthless. Palpatine conquered the galaxy because he craved power, but the First Order may want more than power. They may want revenge on the government, on the people who ended Palpatine's reign, and who failed to stop them from fleeing into hiding.

If we are to fight the First Order, we must have more starships, especially starfighters. We must strengthen our contacts within Incom-FreiTek, Mon Calamari Shipyards, and Slayn & Korpil, in the hope they will supply us with vessels. But we can't rely entirely on our current contacts. We must reach out and form new alliances.

The attached datatape lists our contacts at starship manufacturers, and also contact information and the last-whereabouts for former personnel at defunct manufacturers, such as Koensayr Manufacturing and Kuat Systems Engineering. The datatape also includes list of military surplus wholesalers, starship scrapyards, parts dealers, and recycling centers, all sympathetic to our cause.

I've assigned Admiral Statura to be in charge of ship procurement. If you have information that may help the Admiral procure more ships faster, I trust you will give him your full support. Because if the First Order is preparing to attack the New Republic, the Resistance fleet must be ready to stop them.

◀ Following in the tradition of the brave Rebel Alliance pilots who used small starfighters to combat the Imperial fleet, Resistance pilots use their own fighters against the First Order's massive warships.

T-70 X-WING STARFIGHTER

The successor to the Rebel Alliance's Incom T-65 X-wing starfighter, the Incom-FreiTek T-70 X-wing served the New Republic Defense Fleet for more than two decades. Faster than the T-65, the T-70 is also more heavily armored, and possesses not only sufficient maneuverability to engage TIE fighters in dogfights but also enough firepower to take down capital ships. And whereas the rebels obtained T-65s by any means they could, and typically had to modify the fighters for combat against the Empire, the New Republic had the relative luxury of being able to order new T-70 X-wings directly from authorized manufacturers.

However, a combination of the New Republic's Military Disarmament Act and rampant corruption led to the New Republic granting contracts for T-70 X-wings to only a few well-connected starship manufacturers. After the Republic Navy decided to phase out the T-70 and replace it with the Incom-FreiTek T-85 X-wing, manufacturers continued to produce T-70s for New Republic-allied planetary defense forces, albeit with severely limited production runs due to the Military Disarmament Act.

Anticipating a conflict with the mysterious First Order, New Republic representatives formed the Resistance, and began obtaining starfighters in preparation for war. Because used and decommissioned T-70 X-wing were both available, affordable, and remained highly reliable, Resistance agents discreetly obtained as many T-70s as they could. Eventually, the T-70 X-wing became the signature combat craft of the Resistance's Starfighter Corps.

▲ **Like the T-65B X-wing, the T-70 has excellent maneuverability in atmospheres as well as in outer space.**

◀ **Upgraded sensor systems enabled T-70 X-wing pilots to more easily pass through asteroid fields and similarly hazardous areas.**

▲ Resistance pilot Commander Poe Dameron coated his customized T-70 X-wing with sensor-scattering ferrosphere paint, which helps make his starfighter a more difficult target for enemy aces.

▼ The Incom-FreiTek T-70 X-wing starfighter is more expensive and complex than the First Order's TIE fighters but is also a more versatile combat craft.

SPECIFICATIONS T-70 X-WING STARFIGHTER

MANUFACTURER: Incom-FreiTek
AFFILIATION: New Republic, Resistance
MODEL: T-70 X-wing
CLASS: Starfighter
LENGTH: 12.49 m (41 ft)
WIDTH: 11.26 m (37 ft)
HEIGHT: 1.92 m (6 ft 3 in)
MAXIMUM ACCELERATION: 3,800 G
MEGALIGHT PER HOUR: 110 MGLT
MAXIMUM SPEED (ATMOSPHERE): 1,100 kph (683.5 mph)

ENGINE: Incom-FreiTek 5L5 fusial thrust engines (4)
HYPERDRIVE: Class 1 Incom GBn-682 hyperdrive motivators (4)
SHIELDING: Chempat deflector shield generator
NAVIGATION SYSTEM: Astromech droid
TARGETING SYSTEMS: Fabritech ANq 5.8 tracking computer; IN-622-A "Sightline" holographic imaging system

ARMAMENT: Taim & Bak KX12 laser cannons (4)
ESCAPE CRAFT: Ejector seat
CREW: Pilot (1)
LIFE SUPPORT: Equipped
CONSUMABLES: 1 week
COST: 200,000 credits new; 110,000 used

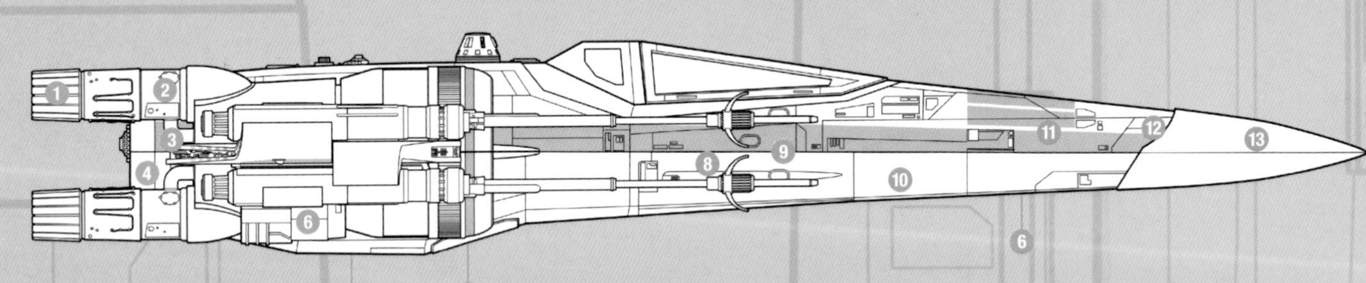

1. Exhaust nozzle
2. Fusial thrust engine
3. Coolant feed
4. Fuel pump
5. Fuel tank
6. Landing gear door
7. Astromech loading door
8. Torpedo launch tube
9. Footholds
10. Repulsorlift
11. Sensor computer
12. Subspace radio
13. Primary sensor array
14. Squadron markings
15. Deflector ducts
16. Deflector shield projectors
17. Titanium alloy hull
18. S-foil servo actuator
19. Hyperdrive
20. Deflector shield generator
21. Astromech droid socket
22. Cockpit canopy
23. Emergency canopy release charge
24. Flight computer
25. Storage access
26. Sensor window
27. Nose cone
28. Engine access panels
29. Underslung blaster cannon (concealed)
30. Laser generator
31. Laser cooling sleeve
32. Magnetic flashback suppressors
33. Laser tip

▶ The T-70's MG7-A launcher fires proton torpedoes that can punch through an enemy ship's deflector shields.

◀ Incom-FreiTek designers and engineers utilized many technological advances to make the T-70 X-wing superior to the T-65B, but kept most components in the same respective sections as the T-65B. Advances in miniaturization enabled Incom-FreiTek to reduce the size of components in the T-70 X-wing's fuselage and create an additional cargo compartment, which pilots typically use for storing survival gear.

14
16
15
17
18
19
21
22
23
24
25
26
27
28
20
29
30
31
32
33

▲ Operating at secret outposts and hangars, Resistance mechanics and flight crews worked in rotating shifts to make sure their T-70 X-wings were always ready for combat.

CUTAWAY T-70 X-WING STARFIGHTER

1. Laser cannon
2. S-foil
3. Deflector ducts
4. Deflector shield generator
5. Deflector shield projector
6. Exhaust nozzle
7. Fusial thrust engine
8. Laser generator heat sink
9. Coolant feed
10. Rear landing gear housing
11. S-foil actuator
12. Hyperdrive
13. Life-support system
14. Fusion chamber
15. Reactant tank
16. Astromech socket
17. BB unit
18. Droid lift platform (bottom loading)
19. Transparisteel canopy
20. Targeting computer
21. Guidenhauser ejection seat
22. Flight controls
23. Emergency canopy release charge
24. Torpedo launch tube
25. Footholds
26. Acceleration compensator
27. Flight computer
28. Storage access panel
29. Forward repulsorlifts
30. Forward landing gear housing
31. Subspace communications antenna
32. Sensor window
33. Primary sensor array
34. Emergency beacon
35. Nose cone
36. Turbo impeller
37. Reactant injector
38. Electromagnetic gyroscope
39. Retro thrusters
40. Maneuvering repulsors
41. Frequency alternator servos
42. Laser cannon charge cells
43. Position marker light
44. Static discharge coupling
45. Laser generator
46. Plasma combination injector
47. Laser cooling sleeve
48. Laser blast condensing channel
49. Magnetic flashback suppressors
50. Laser tip

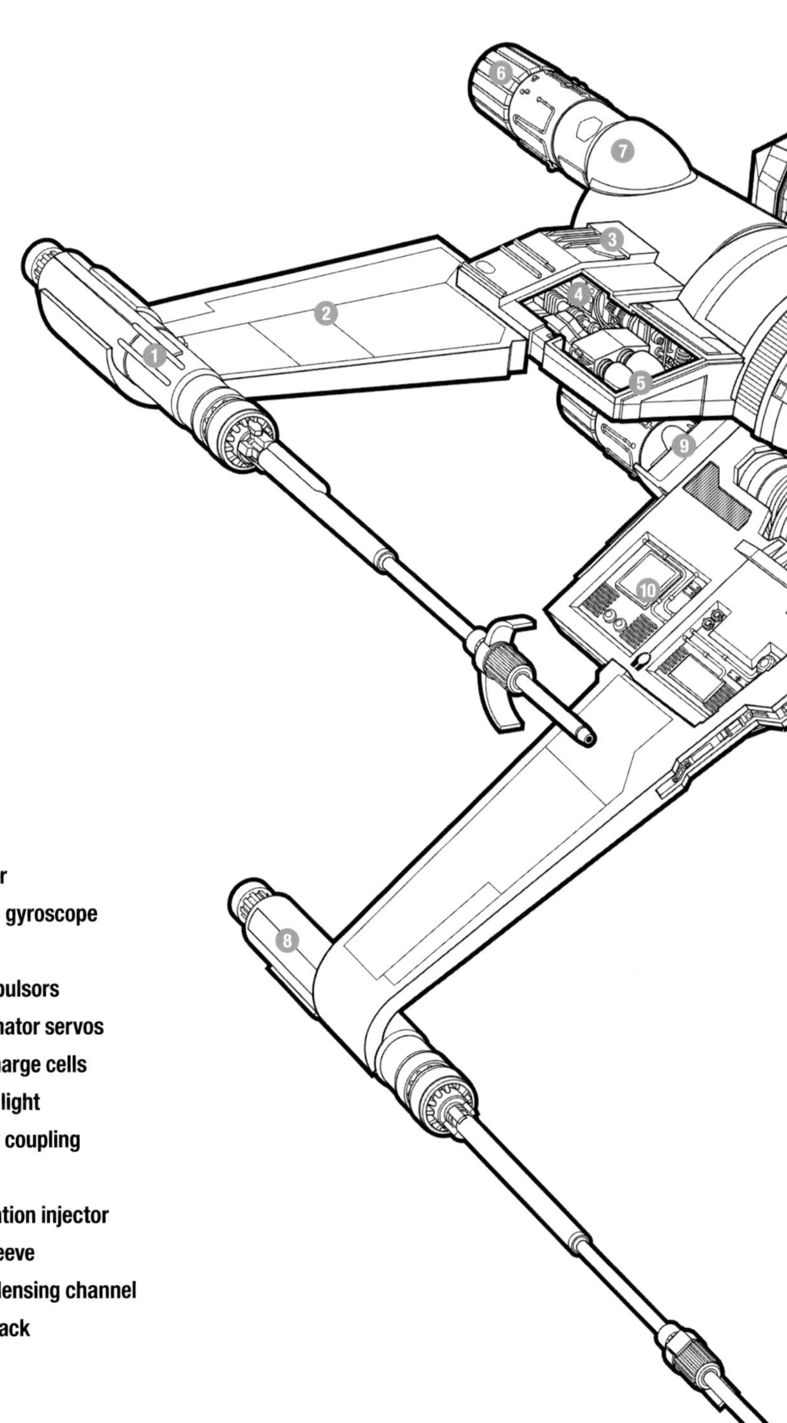

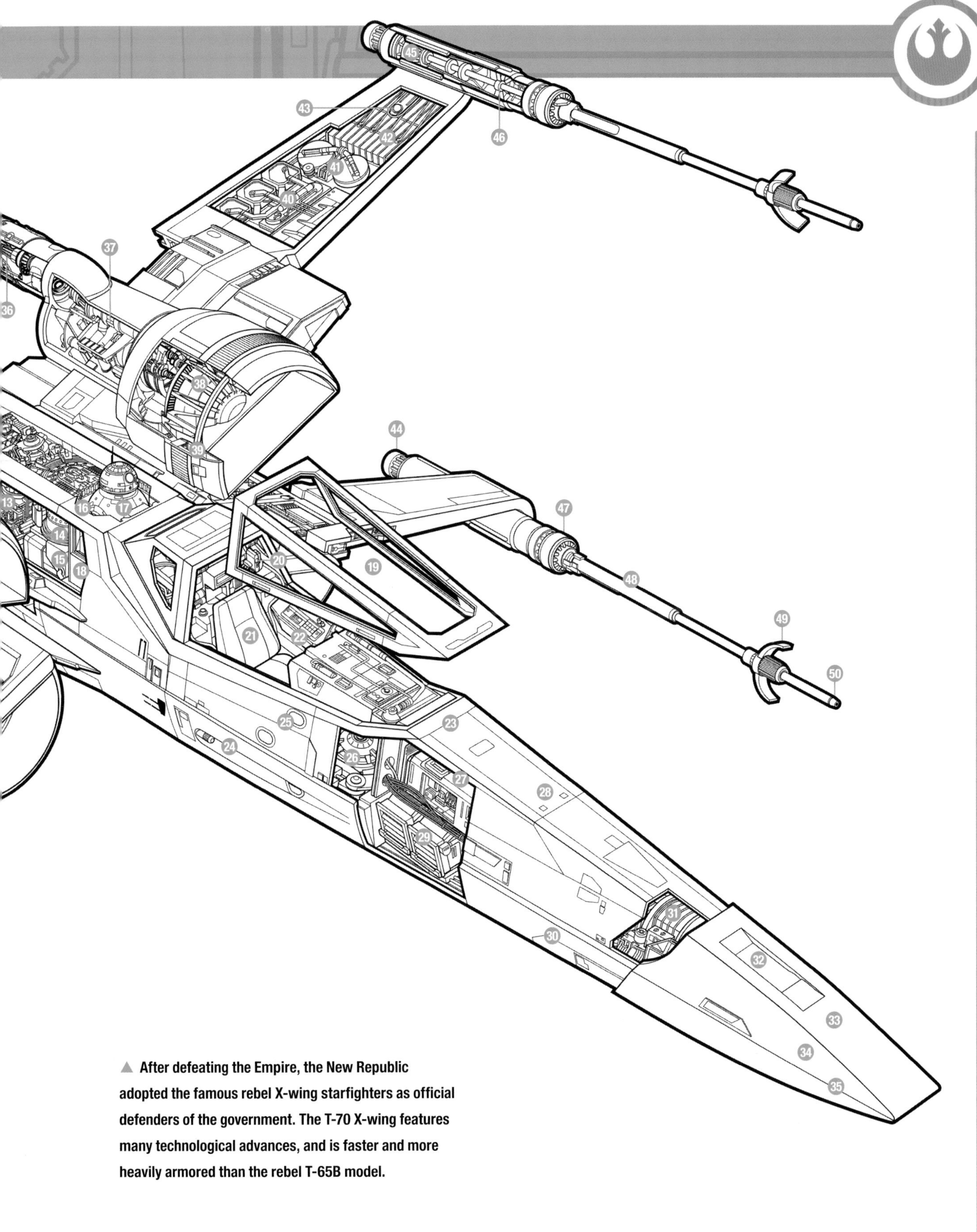

▲ After defeating the Empire, the New Republic adopted the famous rebel X-wing starfighters as official defenders of the government. The T-70 X-wing features many technological advances, and is faster and more heavily armored than the rebel T-65B model.

VIEWS

FRONT 3/4 VIEW

Despite its general resemblance to the T-65B X-wing, the T-70 X-wing's distinctive "split-engines" and streamlined S-foils distinguish the fighter from the T-65B. Incom-FreiTek would retain the advanced split-engine design for the T-70's successor, the T-85 X-wing.

STARBOARD VIEW

Technological advances enabled Incom engineers to make the T-70 X-wing slightly smaller in overall dimensions than the T-65B X-wing. The T-70's shorter length, height, and wingspan contribute to improved maneuverability in both space and atmospheric flights.

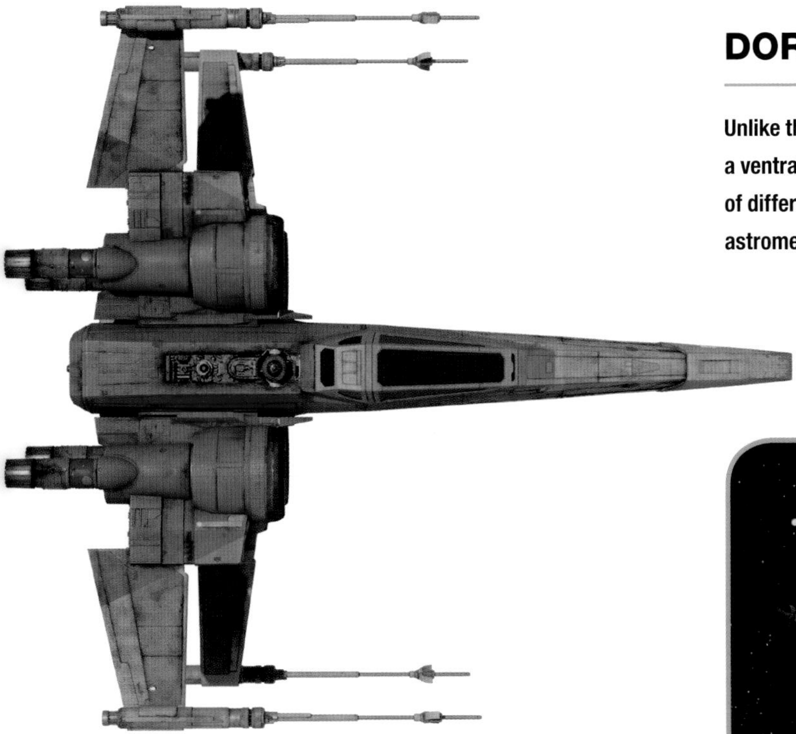

DORSAL AND VENTRAL VIEWS

Unlike the T-65 X-wing's dorsal astromech socket, the T-70 features a ventral astromech socket that provides easier access for a variety of different astromech droids, including R-series and BB-series astromechs manufactured by Industrial Automaton.

FORWARD AND AFT VIEWS

To give himself an edge in combat, Resistance pilot Commander Poe Dameron installed an experimental thrust accelerator pod to his customized T-70's propulsion system.

T-70 X-WING SUBLIGHT ENGINES

Four Incom-FreiTek 5L5 fusial thrust engines give the T-70 X-wing starfighter its speed, but the T-70 owes its great maneuverability to finely calibrated retro thrusters with built-in magnetic gyros, which enable the T-70 to swing in even tighter curves than its nimble predecessor, the T-65B X-wing.

The design and physical shapes of the T-70's engines and Strike foils also factor into improved performance. Unlike the T-65B X-wing's Incom 4L4 fusial thrust engines, which were cylindrical and featured circular retro-thrust nozzles at the fore of each engine, each of the T-70's 5L5 engines is a "split" cylinder. When the T-70's S-foils are stowed in primary cruise mode, the overlapping engines appear to form a pair of single cylindrical engines on either side of the fuselage, making the T-70 resemble one of its earliest design predecessors, the Incom/Subpro Z-95 Headhunter. When the T-70's S-foils are deployed in primary attack mode, the deployment reveals each engine is a split cylinder, fronted by a half circle-shaped retro-thrust nozzle. The reduced surface area of the T-70's nozzles and half-cylinder shape of the engines, combined with technological advancements that allow for smaller but extremely powerful engine components, help make the T-70 faster and more maneuverable than previous X-wing models.

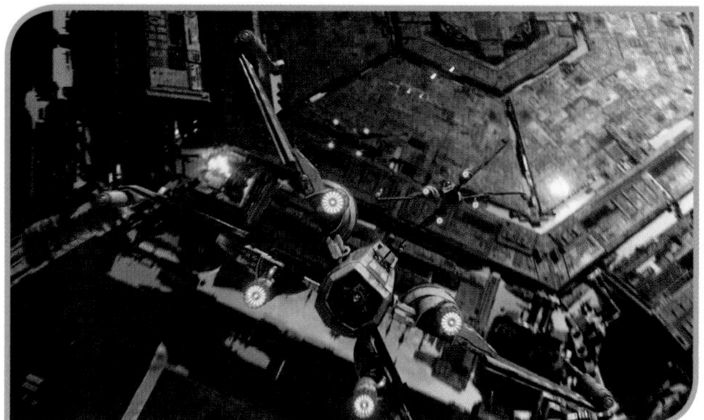

◀ The Incom-FreiTek 5L5 fusial thrust engines were far more energy efficient than either the Incom 4L4 or 4j.4 fusial thrust engines on the Rebel Alliance's T-65B X-wings.

▲ Like previous model X-wing engines, each of the T-70's four 5L5 engines includes a turbo generator that drives a repulsorlift drive adaptor, which gives the T-70 repulsorlift functionality similar to that of a high-performance airspeeder.

▶ With the T-70 X-wing's landing gear deployed, and its S-foils magnetically locked together, the two retro-thrust nozzles at the front of each pair of overlapping 5L5 engines resemble a single cylindrical engine bisected by a horizontal strut.

▼ The Incom-FreiTek 5L5 thrust engines' advanced technology enabled the T-70 X-wing to achieve a standard sublight speed of 110 megalights per hour, an increase of 10 megalights per hour over the Incom T-65 X-wing's standard sublight speed.

SUBLIGHT ENGINE

1. Retro thrusters
2. Electromagnetic gyros
3. Laminar debris extractor
4. Ion stabilizers
5. Hyperdrive motivator
6. Ion recirculator
7. Power converter
8. Field stabilizer
9. Reactant agitator injector
10. Support frame
11. Alluvial damper
12. Fission chamber
13. Turbo impeller
14. Turbo generator
15. Power surge vent
16. Coolant feed

T-70 X-WING COCKPIT AND FLIGHT CONTROLS

The Incom-FreiTek T-70 X-wing starfighter's armored, pressurized cockpit module houses the flight controls, targeting computer, and other essential piloting instruments. Under the hull and at the fore of the cockpit module, a removable liquid-cooled flight computer stores data and translates the movement of the flight controls into adjustments to the direction of the fighter's thrust.

Compared with the intuitive flight controls of the Incom T-65B X-wing starfighter, the Incom-FreiTek T-70 X-wing's controls are largely unchanged. As Incom-FrieTek maintains Incom's longstanding policy to install standardized controls for starfighters, airspeeders, and transports, bush pilots with little or no experience operating spacecraft can quickly and confidently fly the T-70. If necessary, an astromech droid, fitted into the T-70's astromech socket, can operate the starfighter without the aid of the pilot.

▲ The T-70 X-wing's flight control stick includes triggers for weapons.

◀ Resistance pilot Poe Dameron consults the control console within his T-70 X-wing cockpit.

▶ The T-70 X-wing featured an adjustable Fabritech ANq 5.8 tracking computer.

T-70 X-WING CONTROLS

1. Deflector shield control
2. Warning annunciator
3. Shield configuration controls
4. Passive sensors
5. Precision targeting scope
6. Acceleration compensator
7. Display selector knobs
8. Critical system status lights
9. Multifunction flight display
10. S-foil activator
11. Laser fire configuration control
12. Shield status
13. Landing controls
14. Primary computer status monitor
15. Trim adjustment
16. Communications
17. Sensor scramblers
18. Main system circuit breakers

T-70 X-WING WEAPONS AND DEFENSES

The T-70 X-wing's primary weapons are four wing-mounted Taim & Bak KX12 laser cannons. Each S-foil holds power couplings and laser cannon charge cells, which accumulate energy for the cannons. The power couplings guide energy to a cannon's laser generator and plasma combination injector, which direct energy through a laser cooling sleeve and laser blast condensing channel. Each cannon's long barrel increases laser bolt stability and range before a laser-blaster converter discharges the laser bolts. Like the T-65 X-wing, the T-70 X-wing can open its S-foils to maximize the four cannons' field of fire, and shed waste heat during combat.

Unlike the T-65 X-wing, which was typically equipped with two Krupx MG7 torpedo launchers that held up to three proton torpedoes each, the T-70 X-wing is equipped with a single Krupx MG7-A torpedo launcher that holds eight miniaturized proton torpedoes. Quick-change magazines allow pilots to swap out torpedoes with other payloads, including concussion missiles or mag-pulse warheads. The MG7-A torpedo launcher is also a detachable unit, one of several modular secondary weapon pods that allow rebel crews to easily replace the launcher with other weapons, such as additional laser cannons. The torpedo launcher is located in the underside of the fuselage, almost directly below the cockpit, in a compartment large enough to hold spent torpedo casings. Quick-change magazines allow pilots to swap torpedoes with other payloads, such as concussion missiles or mag-pulse warheads.

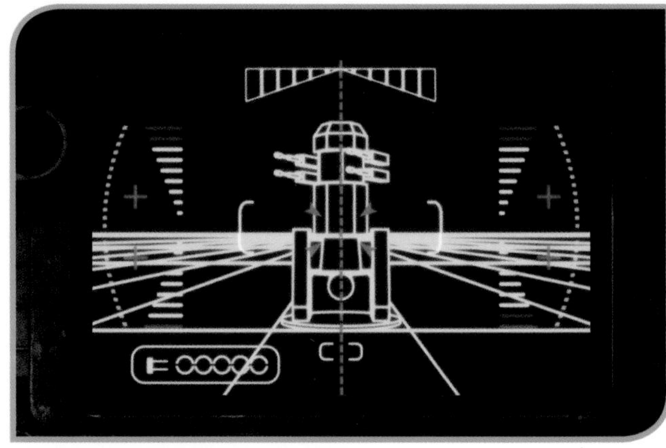

▲ The T-70 X-wing's IN-622-A "Sightline" holographic imaging system displays targets and range data.

◀ Just like its predecessor, the T-70 X-wing has powerful wingtip cannons that can fire in single, dual, or quad mode.

UNDERSLUNG BLASTER CANNON

1. Wing interior compartment
2. Outer wing doors
3. Power cables
4. Gas lines
5. Hydraulic swivel mount
6. Emitter nozzle
7. Heat vents and cooling fins
8. Barrel extending rail
9. Targeting sensor
10. Ship interlink processor
11. Power converter
12. Gas conversion enabler (XCiter)
13. Actuating module

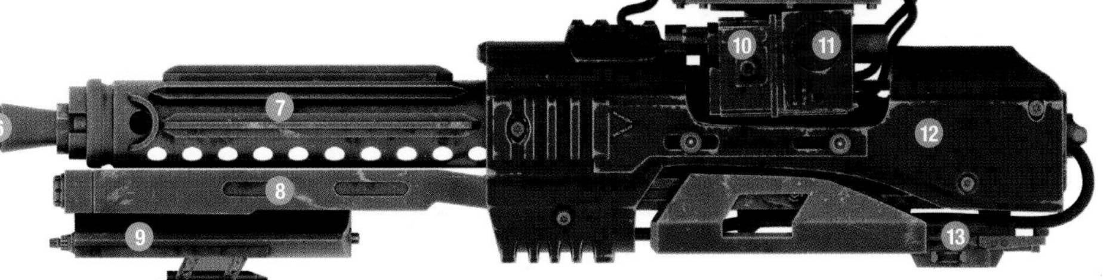

▲ Mounted to the T-70 X-wing's dorsal hull, a rotatable BlasTech Ax-190-B blaster cannon provides rearward defense against enemy fighters.

▶ The T-70 X-wing features an automated computer targeting system that controls an undercarriage-mounted blaster cannon.

T-85 X-WING

The Incom-FreiTek T-70 X-wing starfighter had been in service to the New Republic Defense Fleet for more than two decades when Fleet Admiral Gial Ackbar realized that most T-70s were overdue for technical and mechanical upgrades. Anticipating that the aging starfighters would require additional maintenance, modifications, and repairs within five years, Ackbar proposed that the Republic Navy should commission Incom-FreiTek to design a prototype for a next-generation model of the X-wing.

The result was the T-85 X-wing, which maintained certain design aspects of the T-70, including S-foils that held "split-cylinder" retro thrusters with built-in electromagnetic gyros, and also the variable-configuration droid socket that accommodated a variety of astromechs. Improvements included more powerful and energy-efficient fusial thrust engines, and also improved flight systems that enabled a pilot to more easily steer the fighter through loops and rolls. Advances in laser cannon technology negated the need for magnetic flashback suppressors on the T-85 laser cannons but some Republic Navy pilots—doubtful about the new technology—insisted on installing customized suppressors as a precaution.

When the First Order destroyed the Hosnian system, they not only atomized countless lifeforms on five worlds but also most of the New Republic Defense Fleet, including most T-85 X-wings in the Republic Navy. Desperate to prevent the First Order from committing further atrocities, the Resistance scrambled to acquire any available starfighters. Although they managed to obtain more T-70 X-wings, they may never again see the T-85.

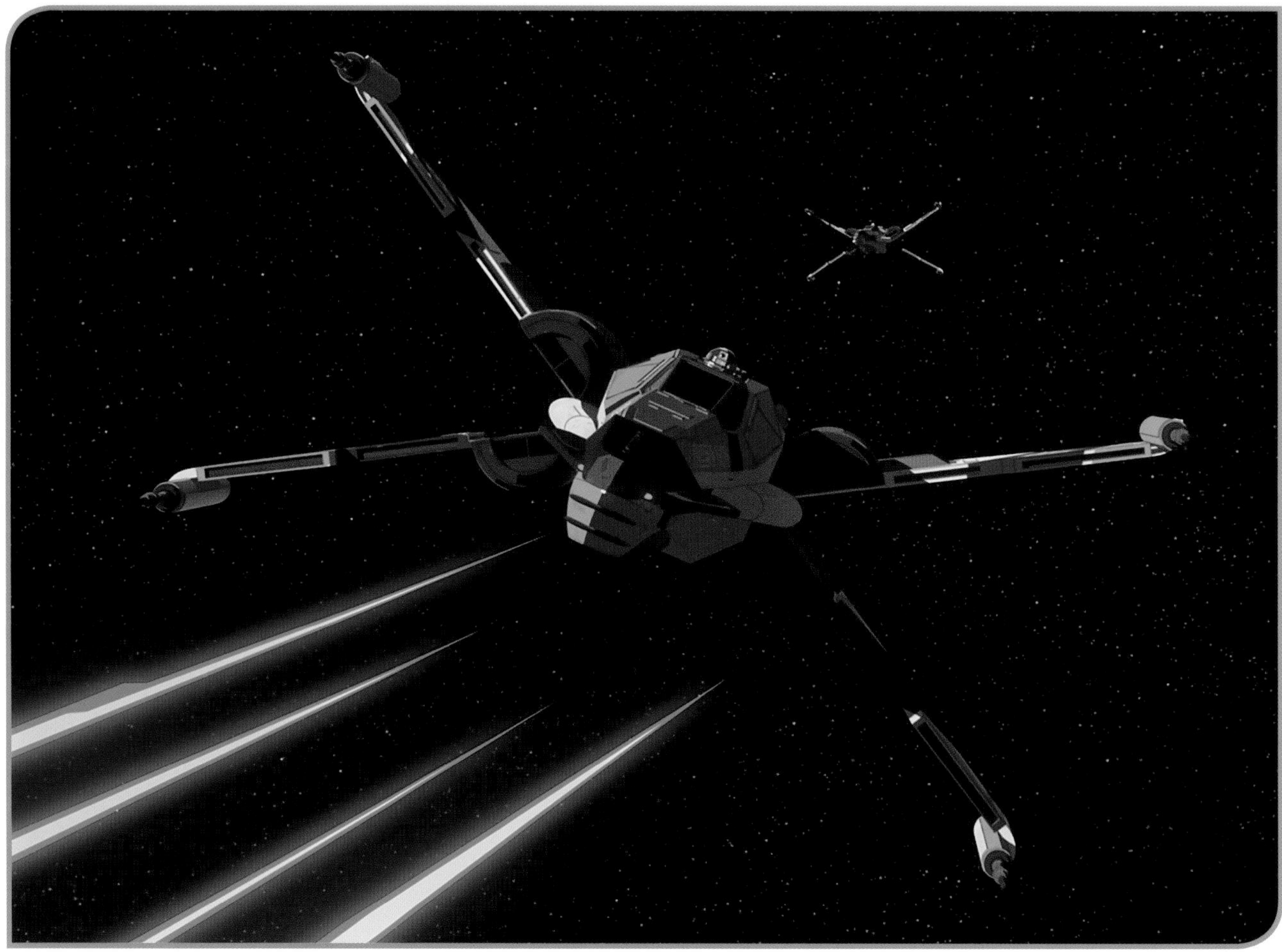

▲ Incom-FreiTek designed the T-85 X-wing with a distinctive nose to house an exotic sensor suite that helped pilots to be better prepared when they encountered actual or potential threats.

◀ The New Republic Navy used T-85 X-wing starfighters to maintain peace and defend well-traveled space lanes against pirates.

▶ Several months before the First Order destroyed most of the New Republic Defense Fleet, pilot Poe Dameron and his allies flew T-85 X-wings for the Defense Fleet's Starfighter Corps.

SPECIFICATIONS T-85 X-WING

MANUFACTURER: Incom-FreiTek
AFFILIATION: New Republic
MODEL: T-85 X-wing
CLASS: Starfighter
LENGTH: 15.68 m (51ft 5 in)
WIDTH: 13.65 m (44 ft 9 in)
HEIGHT: 2.7 m (8 ft 10 in)
MAXIMUM ACCELERATION: 3, 800 G
MEGALIGHT PER HOUR: 120 MGLT
MAXIMUM SPEED (ATMOSPHERE): 1,300 kph (808 mph)

ENGINE: Incom-FreiTek 5L9 fusial thrust engines (4)
HYPERDRIVE: Class 1
SHIELDING: Chempat deflector shield projector
NAVIGATION SYSTEM: Astromech droid
TARGETING SYSTEMS: Fabritech ANr 1.3 tracking computer; IN-630-B "Sightline" holographic imaging system

ARMAMENT: Taim & Bak KX14 laser cannons; Krupx MG7-B proton torpedo launchers
ESCAPE CRAFT: Ejector seat
CREW: Pilot (1)
LIFE SUPPORT: Equipped
CONSUMABLES: 1 week
COST: 220,000 credits new; 140,000 used

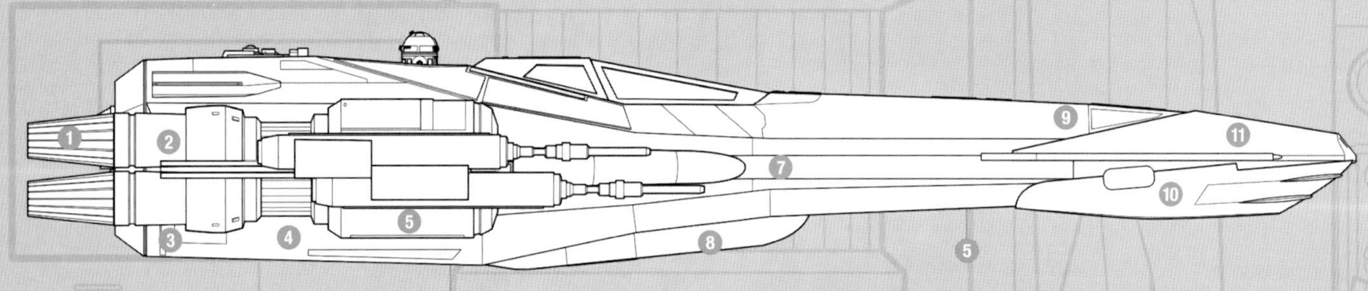

1 Exhaust nozzle
2 Fusial thrust engine
3 Fuel pump
4 Fuel tank
5 Landing gear door
6 Cargo bay door
7 Torpedo launch tube
8 Repulsorlift
9 Subspace radio
10 Sensor computer
11 Primary sensor array
12 Thrust controls jets
13 Deflector shield projectors
14 Titanium alloy hull
15 Service cover
16 S-foil servo actuator
17 Hyperdrive
18 Deflector shield generator
19 Astromech droid socket
20 Cockpit canopy
21 Emergency canopy release charge
22 Flight computer
23 Sensor window
24 Nose cone
25 Engine access panels
26 Main cooling plates
27 Laser generator
28 Laser cooling sleeve
29 Magnetic flashback suppressors
30 Laser tip

▲ Resistance Commander Poe Dameron and the astromech droid BB-8 met during Dameron's service with the New Republic Navy, when he was in command of the T-85 X-wing pilots in Rapier Squadron.

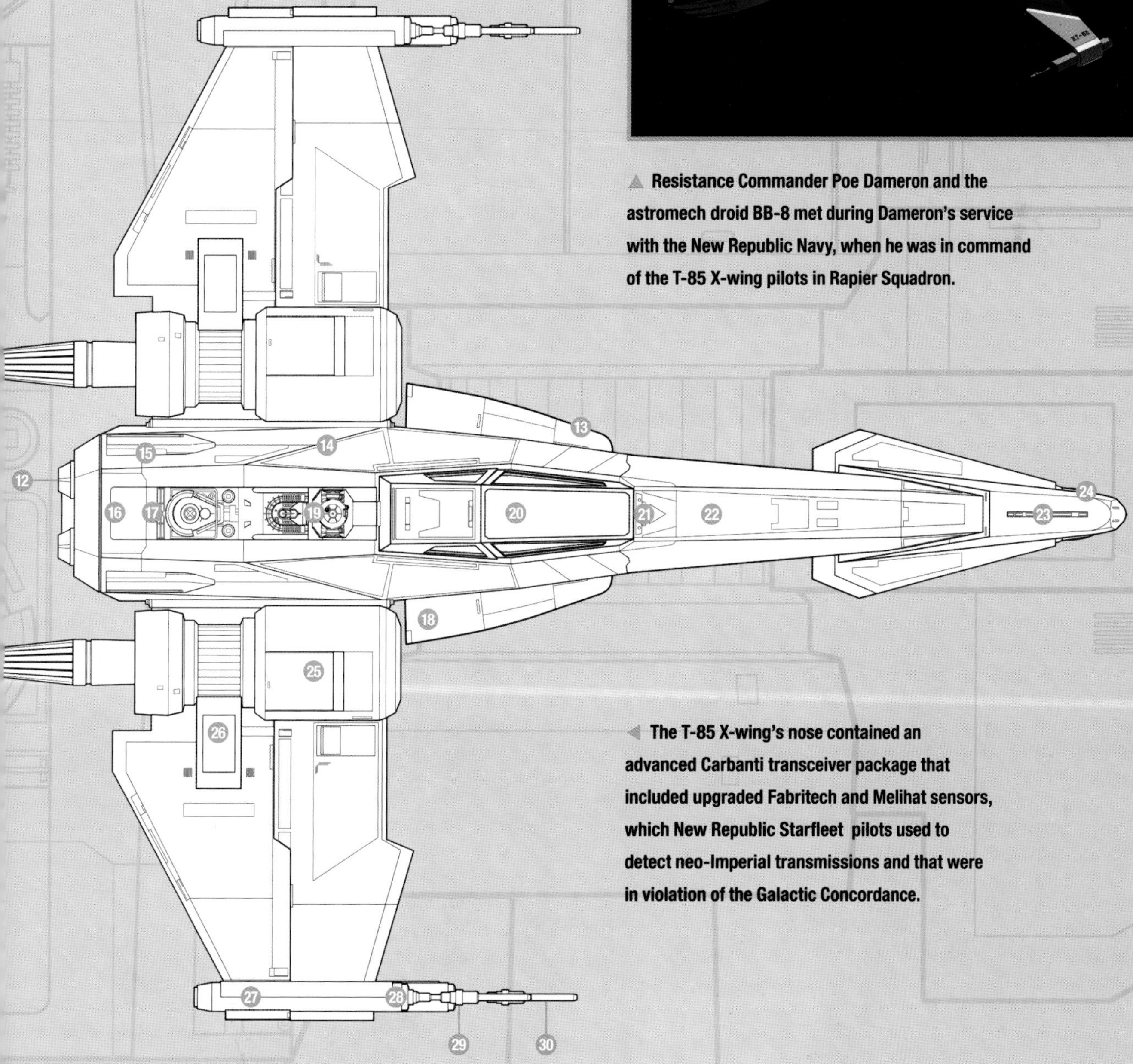

◄ The T-85 X-wing's nose contained an advanced Carbanti transceiver package that included upgraded Fabritech and Melihat sensors, which New Republic Starfleet pilots used to detect neo-Imperial transmissions and that were in violation of the Galactic Concordance.

RZ-2 A-WING INTERCEPTOR

Although the RZ-1 A-wing interceptor was among the fastest starfighters in the galaxy and helped the Rebel Alliance defeat the Imperial armada at the Battle of Endor, the RZ-1 was also notorious for its overly sensitive control system, problematic laser-cannon swivel mounts, and frequent breakdowns. At the urging of veteran rebel pilots and mechanics, the New Republic commissioned Kuat Systems Engineering to develop a revamped A-wing interceptor. After pilots successfully tested Kuat's prototype, Kuat began production of the RZ-2 A-wing interceptor for the New Republic Defense Fleet.

Despite obvious similarities to the RZ-1 A-wing, the RZ-2 A-wing has a longer and more streamlined frame that gives the fighter greater speed than its predecessor, and incorporates numerous field-tested refinements for better control and performance. Because the RZ-2 A-wing was as stealthy as it was fast and well armed, it was ideal for "hit-and-fade" missions against enemy targets. The Republic Navy frequently relied on the RZ-2 for long-range reconnaissance missions and combating space pirates.

After the New Republic's Military Disarmament Act cut production of RZ-2 A-wings to a minimum, the Resistance managed to acquire decommissioned A-wings to bolster its tiny fleet. With its advanced weapons technology and incredible speed, the RZ-2 A-wing is perfectly suited for rapid strikes on capital ships, but the Resistance must use their few A-wings wisely and sparingly if they are to defeat the First Order.

▼ Kuat Systems Engineering supplied Resistance flight crews and their astromech droid assistants with specialized tools to maintain and repair the RZ-2 A-wing.

▼ Located behind the A-wing's cockpit, a Rseik Hullspace F2E "Energy Armor" deflector shield generator uses excess energy from the engines to project a protective bubble around the craft.

▶ Operating under the call sign Blue Leader, Tallissan "Tallie" Lintra commanded Blue Squadron, of RZ-2 A-wing interceptors in the Resistance Starfighter Corps.

SPECIFICATIONS RZ-2 A-WING INTERCEPTOR

MANUFACTURER: Kuat Systems Engineering
AFFILIATION: New Republic, Resistance
MODEL: RZ-2 A-wing
CLASS: Starfighter
LENGTH: 7.68 m (25.2 ft)
WIDTH: 4.62 m (15.16 ft)
HEIGHT: 2.02 m (6.63 ft)
MAXIMUM ACCELERATION: 5,200 G
MEGALIGHT PER HOUR: 125 MGLT
MAXIMUM SPEED (ATMOSPHERE): 1,350 kph

ENGINE: Novaldex K-88 "Event Horizon" sublight engines
HYPERDRIVE: Class 1; Incom GBk-885 hyperdrive motivators (2)
SHIELDING: Rseik Hullspace 2e deflector shield generator
NAVIGATION SYSTEM: Microaxial LpL-849 flight controller
TARGETING SYSTEMS: Pallas "Crosshairs" 98j precision holo-targeter; Fabritech ANs-9e targeting sensor array

ARMAMENT: Zija GO-4 laser cannons (2); Dymek HM-22 concussion missile launchers (2)
ESCAPE CRAFT: Ejector seat
CREW: Pilot (1)
LIFE SUPPORT: Equipped
CONSUMABLES: 1 week
COST: 190,000 New Republic credits new; 115,000 used (military requisition charges)

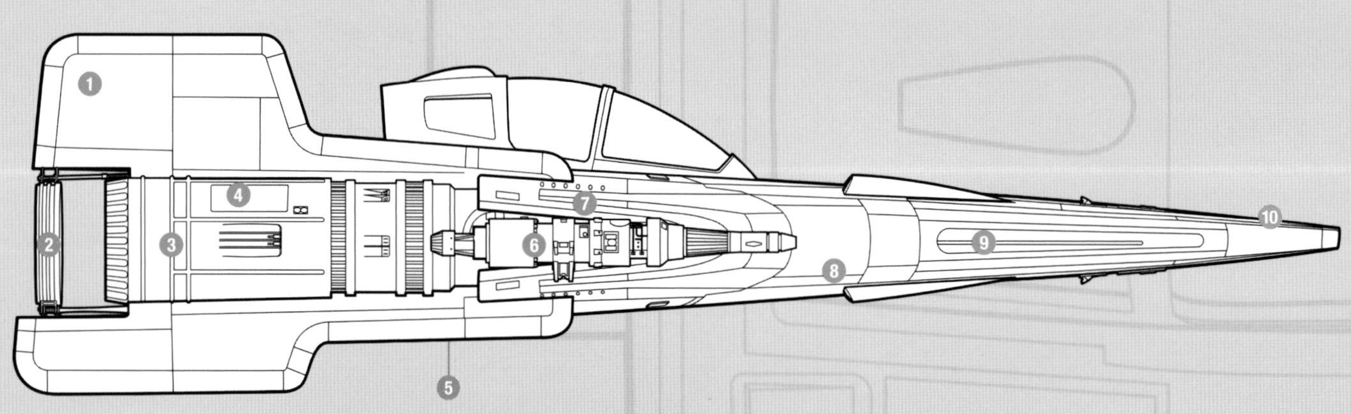

1. Adjustable stabilizers
2. Thrust vector control
3. Sublight engine
4. Engine access panel
5. Miniaturized Hyperdrive
6. Laser cannon
7. Laser cannon charge cells
8. Concussion-missile magazine
9. Missile launch tube
10. Reinforced front wedge
11. Thrust control jets
12. Fusion reactor exhaust
13. Miniaturized fusion reactor
14. Laser cannon swivel mounting
15. Gyro-stabilizing unit (concealed)
16. Deflector shield generator
17. Cockpit deflector shield projector
18. Cockpit canopy
19. Cargo compartment
20. Deflector shield projectors
21. Cloakeye sensor jammer
22. Maintenance access hatch
23. Targeting sensor array
24. Towing slot

Inside the Novaldex K-88 sublight engines, cryogenic power tubes fuel the two enormous Klyd-Marro 67e fusion cores that provide massive thrust to achieve high speeds for the RZ-2 A-wing.

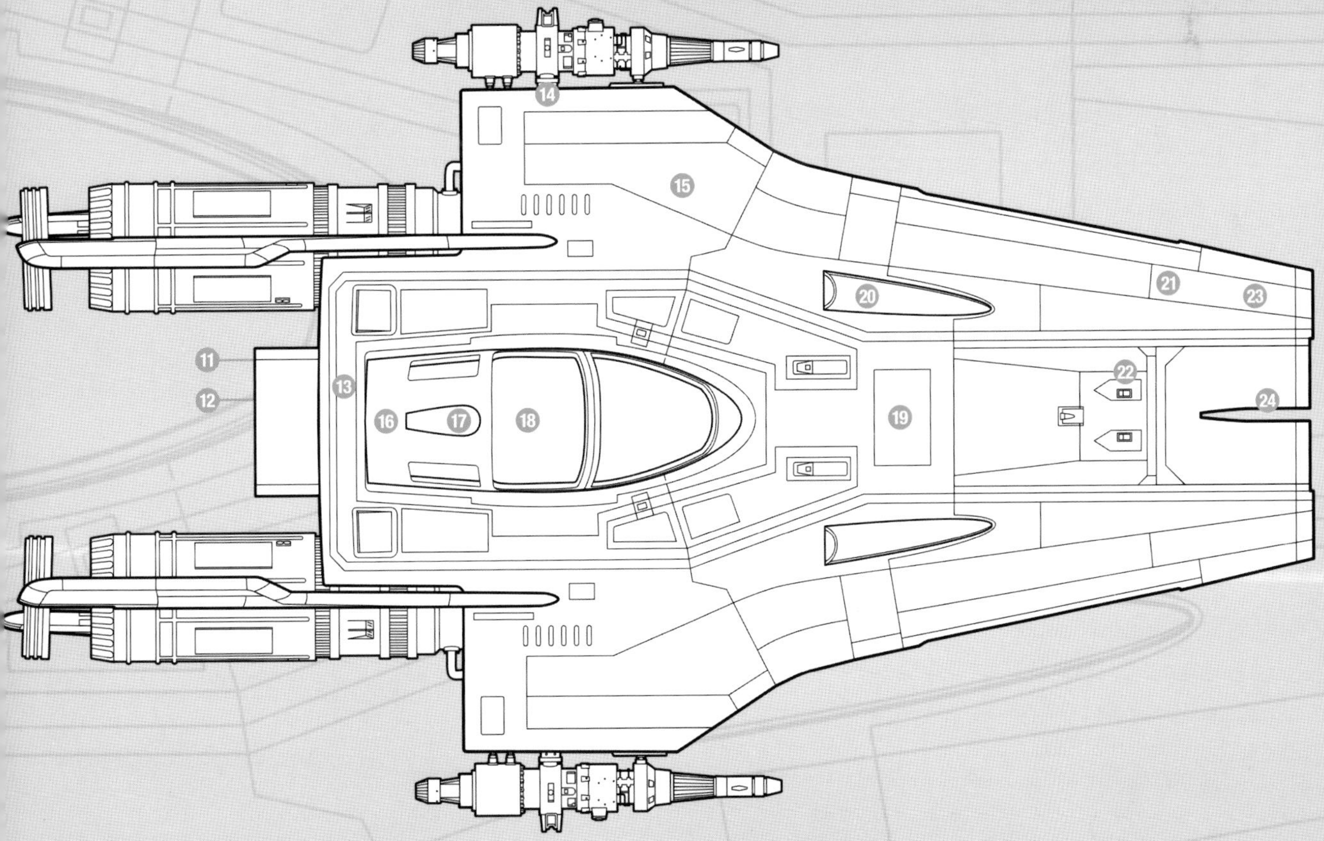

An A-wing's avionics system re-tunes the electromagnetic noise created by the Novaldex engines and broadcasts wide-spectrum interference that blinds multi-spectral imagers. While larger ships with more sophisticated sensors are immune to this jamming, smaller ships like TIE fighters find it difficult to track an A-wing or even call for aid when they are in its vicinity.

VIEWS

FRONT 3/4 VIEW

Routine maintenance checks for the RZ-2 A-wing require considerably less time than the Alliance-era RZ-1, but access panels at various locations on the hull allow technicians and mechanics to easily repair the most vital systems.

STARBOARD VIEW

Compared with the RZ-1 A-wing, the RZ-2 A-wing has a greater length and width but smaller height. Advances in miniaturization technology prompted Kuat Systems Engineering to utilize smaller deflector-shield components, which allowed Kuat to truncate the generator cowling behind the RZ-2's cockpit canopy.

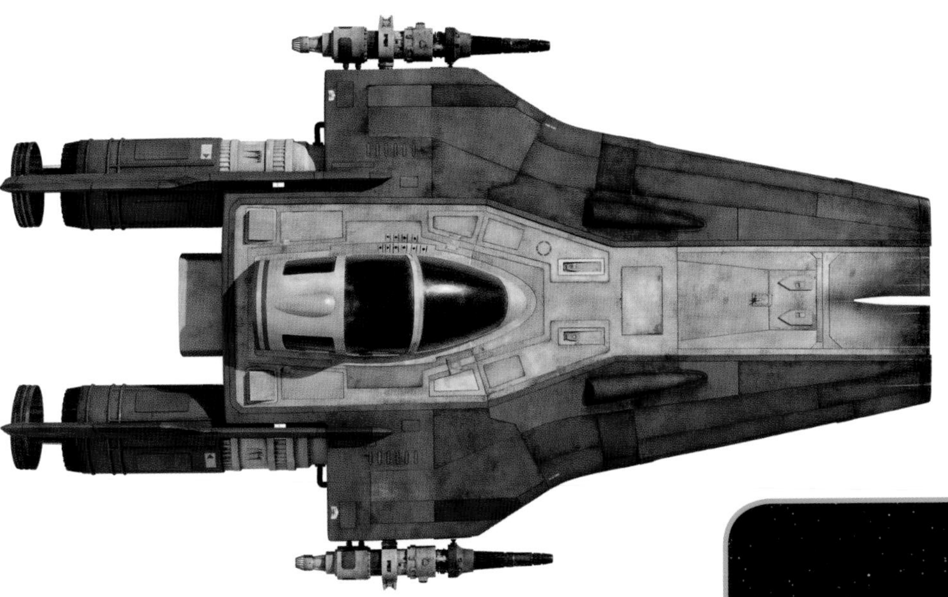

DORSAL AND VENTRAL VIEWS

Kuat engineers installed Incom GBk-885 hyperdrive motivators in each of the RZ-2 A-wing's sublight engine nacelles to initiate jumps to lightspeed.

FORWARD AND AFT VIEWS

Like the RZ-1 A-wing interceptor, the RZ-2 A-wing's frame cannot accommodate an astromech droid. Because flying a fighter without an astromech poses a challenge for many pilots, the Resistance allows only their most skilled pilots to fly A-wings.

RZ-2 A-WING COCKPIT AND FLIGHT CONTROLS

When the New Republic Defense Fleet commissioned Kuat Systems Engineering to design a new A-wing interceptor, a number of veteran pilots recalled the RZ-1 A-wing's cramped cockpit, and wondered if Kuat engineers could create a cockpit that was even slightly larger without compromising speed or maneuverability. Because Kuat designers gave the RZ-2 A-wing a greater length than the RZ-1, they were able to increase legroom in the cockpit, a detail that impressed the veteran pilots.

Despite the additional length and other subtle changes, the RZ-2 A-wing is something of a throwback to Kuat's original R-22 starfighter in that the cockpit has a transparisteel canopy that opens and closes by way of an aft-mounted pneumatic hinge. Although Kuat considered the rebel-engineered canopy system that slid forward and backward on tracks to open and close, Kuat determined that the hinged mechanism was easier to operate and less expensive to maintain.

The RZ-2 A-wing's state-of-the art flight systems include a Microaxial LpL-849 flight controller and a Pallas "Crosshairs" 98j precision holo-targeter. The flight controller assists the pilot with numerous maneuvers while pursuing or evading targets. One strategy, known as the "A-wing Slash," calls for slower fighters like X-wings to engage with and distract a group of enemies before A-wings dive into the battle and make a devastating surprise attack.

▲ **Kuat Systems Engineering simplified the RZ-2 A-wing's controls for faster ignition and better control of weapons systems.**

▼ **Resistance crews marked flight decks to ensure personnel stayed clear of the RZ-2 A-wing's aft when pilots fired the engines.**

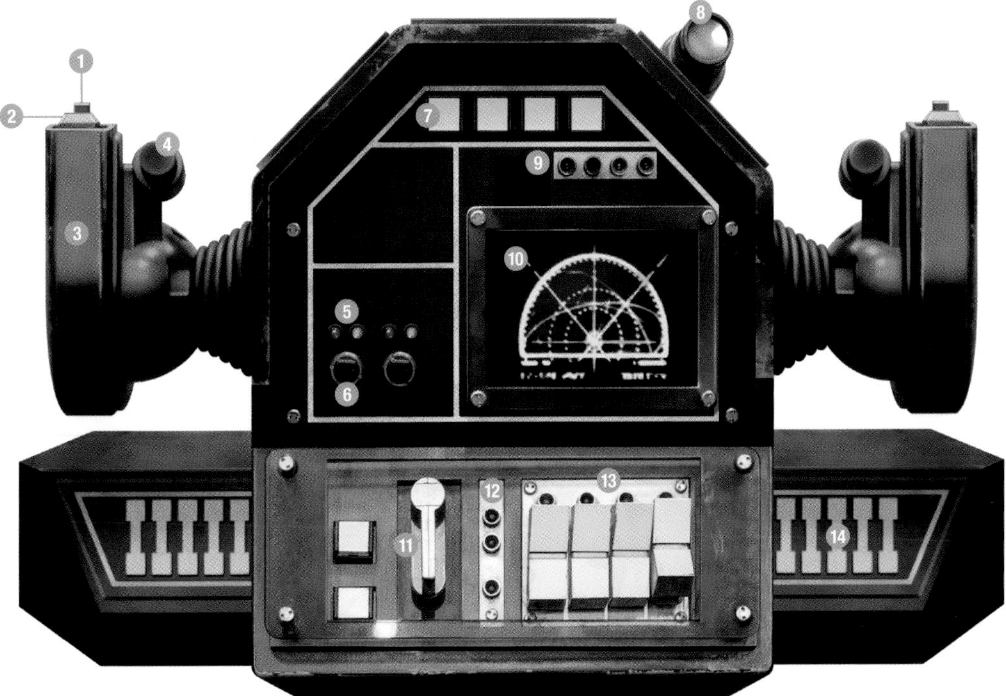

▶ Instead of replicating the RZ-1 A-wing's control console and its various circular scopes, Kuat gave the RZ-2 A-wing an entirely new console with a large rectangular monitor that neatly displayed ship status, flight and speed indicators, and sensor data.

RZ-2 A-WING CONTROLS

1. Safety
2. Weapons trigger
3. Control handle
4. System menu selector
5. Engine status indicators
6. Engine ignition
7. Weapons arming switches
8. Master caution indicator
9. Display mode indicator
10. Display monitor
11. Communications
12. Landing gear indicator
13. Deflector shields
14. Air scrubbers
15. Life support controls

▶ Like Kuat's original R-22 starfighter prototype, the RZ-2 features a pneumatically hinged cockpit canopy.

RZ-2 A-WING WEAPONS AND DEFENSES

When Kuat Systems Engineering designers and engineers began working on the RZ-2 A-wing interceptor prototype for the New Republic Defense Fleet, their goals included fabricating improved swivel-mount emplacements for the laser cannons to prevent the problems that caused the RZ-1 A-wing's cannons to jam. After they broke down a modified RZ-1 A-wing, analyzed the craft's Borstel Galactic Defense RG-9 laser cannons and targeting computer systems, and interviewed veteran rebel pilots and mechanics, they pinpointed numerous problems that discouraged them from considering Borstel-manfactured weapons for the new A-wing.

The RZ-2 A-wing's primary weapons are two swivel-mounted Zija GO-4 laser cannons. To prevent the cannons from jamming when rotated to fire at targets behind the fighter, Kuat designed entirely new mounts that are linked with refined and more reliable port and starboard gyro stabilizers that can rotate between the ship's front and rear arcs. Kuat also equipped the RZ-2 A-wing with two Dymek HM-22 concussion missile launchers, each loaded with a six-missile magazine.

A Fabritech ANs-9e forward sensor, targeting sensor array, and navigation sensors collect and feed raw data about surrounding spacecraft and objects into the flight and targeting computers. An advanced CloakEye sensor jammer housed in front of the cockpit canopy serves to impede detection, and works in conjunction with an Irilliad "Blinder" 4B2 jamming array that broadcasts data bursts to disrupt enemy sensors.

TORPEDOS AND MISSILES

1. Miniaturized MG7-A proton torpedo
2. Armor penetrating housing
3. Proton warhead
4. Guidance gyro
5. Armor power shell
6. Concussion missile
7. Targeting sensors
8. Concussion warhead
9. Shielded guidance computer
10. Propellant body
11. Thrust control unit
12. Launch initiator

▼ As an interceptor, the A-wing's mission profile typically requires concussion missiles for ship-to-ship combat. The standardized launchers will also accept miniaturized proton torpedoes more commonly used in the X and Y-wings.

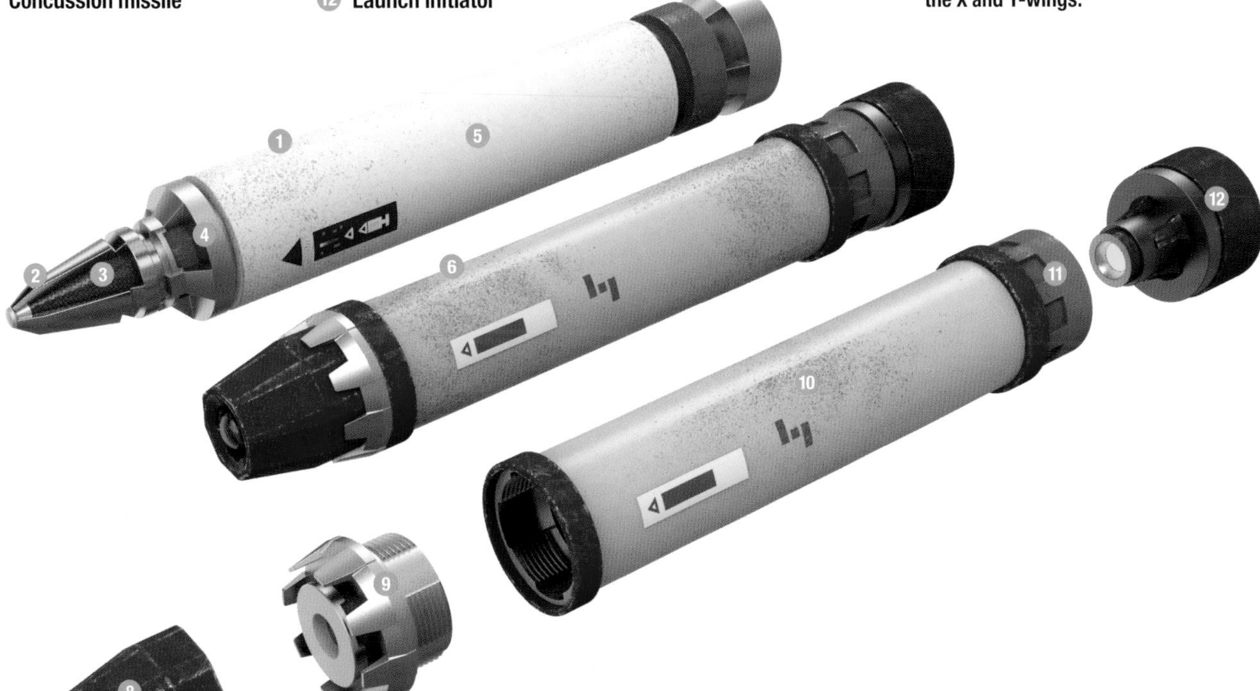

▼ RZ-2 A-wings served as defensive escorts to the Resistance's fleet of MG-100 StarFortress bombers during assaults on First Order capital ships.

◀ Unlike the jury-rigged swivel mounts that rebel mechanics created for the RZ-1 A-wing, the Resistance's RZ-2 A-wings featured trouble-free swivel mounts authorized by Kuat Systems Engineeering.

BTA-NR2 Y-WING STARFIGHTER

Although Koensayr Manufacturing's BTL-B Y-wing fighter-bomber became a mainstay of the Republic Navy during the Clone Wars, Koensayr failed to obtain any substantial government contracts after the Galactic Republic gave way to the Galactic Empire. Eventually, the Alliance to Restore the Republic began using stripped-down decommissioned BTL-B and BTL-A4 Y-wings to combat the Empire. By the time the Alliance defeated the Empire, most operational Y-wings were well over twenty years old, and were skeletons of the original Clone Wars-era armored models.

After the Alliance transitioned to become the New Republic, Koensayr ultimately embraced its role in galactic revolution by restarting the Y-wing product line with the BTA-NR2 Y-wing. Because many potential buyers regarded the "rebel Y-wing" as more venerable than the original BTL-B stock model, and also because Koensayr knew that most customers preferred customizable starships to strictly standardized models, Koensayr decided that the BTA-NR2 Y-wing should emulate the rebel-modified BTL-A4, but offered customers stylized "replica" armor plating as an option. Proudly promoting the new Y-wing as "the starfighter that broke the Empire's back," Koensayr marketed the BTA-NR2 as a patrol and planetary-defense craft in New Republic star systems. Like other starship manufacturers that had contracts with the New Republic Defense Fleet, Koensayr followed guidelines to comply with the Galactic Concordance's regulations and restrictions for specific weapons on "peacekeeping" starfighters.

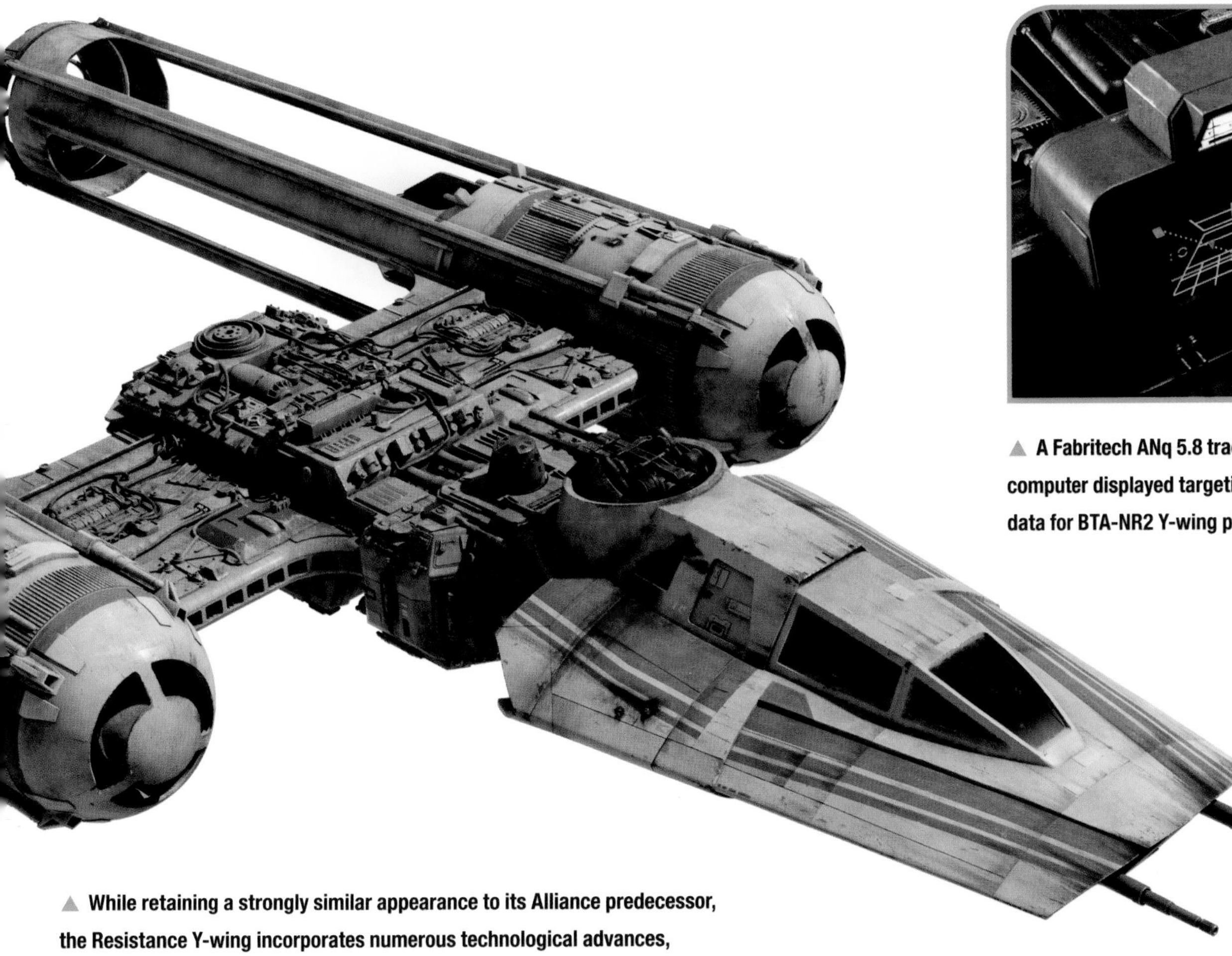

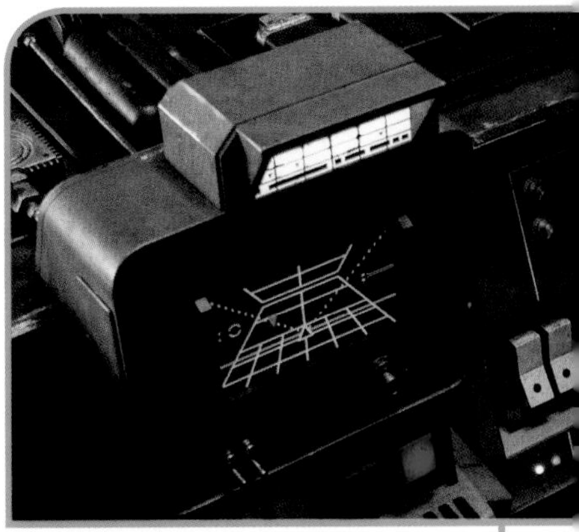

▲ A Fabritech ANq 5.8 tracking computer displayed targeting data for BTA-NR2 Y-wing pilots.

▲ While retaining a strongly similar appearance to its Alliance predecessor, the Resistance Y-wing incorporates numerous technological advances, including stronger deflector shields and more sophisticated sensors.

◀ Resistance flight crews equipped New Republic Defense Fleet BTA-NR2 Y-wing patrol crafts with ordnance launchers.

▶ Koensayr installed upgraded controls and flight-monitoring systems around the Guidenhauser ejector seat inside the BTA-NR2 Y-wing's cockpit.

SPECIFICATIONS BTA-NR2 Y-WING STARFIGHTER

MANUFACTURER: Koensayr Manufacturing
AFFILIATION: New Republic, Resistance
MODEL: BTA-NR2 Y-wing
CLASS: Starfighter/patrol craft
LENGTH: 18.17 m (59 ft 7 in)
WIDTH: 8.78 m (28 ft 10 in)
HEIGHT: 2.85 m (9 ft 4 in)
MAXIMUM ACCELERATION: 2,750 G
MEGALIGHT PER HOUR: 80 MGLT
MAXIMUM SPEED (ATMOSPHERE): 1,050 kph (652 mph)

ENGINE: Koensayr R750 ion jet engine (2)
HYPERDRIVE: Class 1 Koensayr R400-H
SHIELDING: Chempat deflector shield generator
NAVIGATION SYSTEM: Astromech droid
TARGETING SYSTEMS: Fabritech ANq 5.8 tracking computer
ARMAMENT: Taim & Bak IX4-B laser cannons (2); ArMek SW-9 ion cannons (2); Arakyd Flex Tube proton torpedo launchers (2); proton bombs and torpedoes

ESCAPE CRAFT: Ejector seat
CREW: Pilot (1); astromech droid (1)
LIFE SUPPORT: Equipped
CONSUMABLES: 1 week
COST: 185,000 credits new; 95,000 used

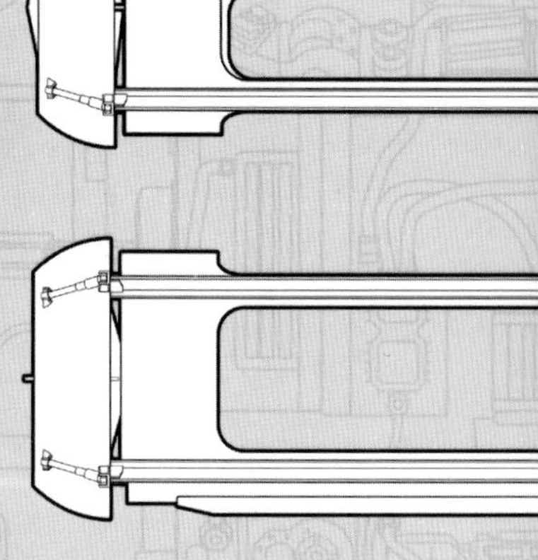

◀ Compared with the BTL-A4 Y-wing's rebel-modified Koensayr R200 ion jet engines, the BTA-NR2 Y-wing's Koensayr R750 ion jet engines are more robust, offer greater speed, and require less maintenance.

1. Support pylons
2. Heavy ion jet turbines
3. Ship-to-ship photonics comm system
4. Long-range targeting sensor array
5. Astromech droid socket
6. Neck repulsorlift
7. Automated turret computer systems
8. Torpedo launch tube position (optional)
9. Laser tip
10. Electromagnetic gyros
11. Main power cell
12. Wing repulsorlift
13. Cooling intakes
14. Heat vents
15. Deflector shield generator
16. Deflector ducts
17. Hyperdrive tachyon exhaust
18. Hyperdrive sequencer
19. Deflector shield projectors
20. Main coolant pump
21. Cockpit pod ejectors
22. Life support equipment
23. Titanium-reinforced Alusteel hull
24. Squadron markings
25. Ion cannon turret
26. Cockpit canopy
27. Vectral ring
28. Exhaust nozzle

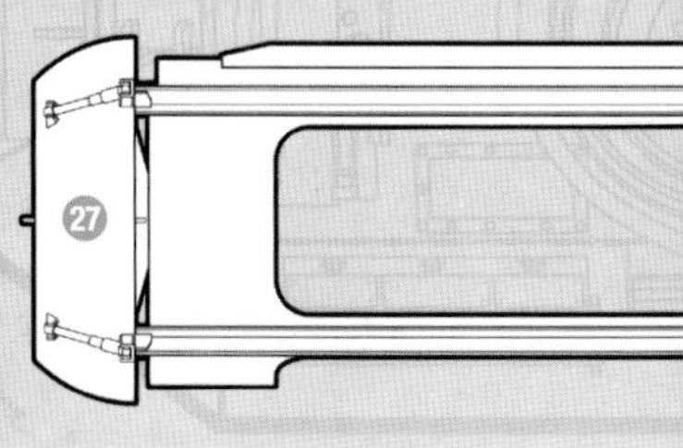

▶ Tucked into its socket behind the Y-wing's cannon turret, an Industrial Automaton R5-series astromech droid monitors the starfighter's flight and weapons systems.

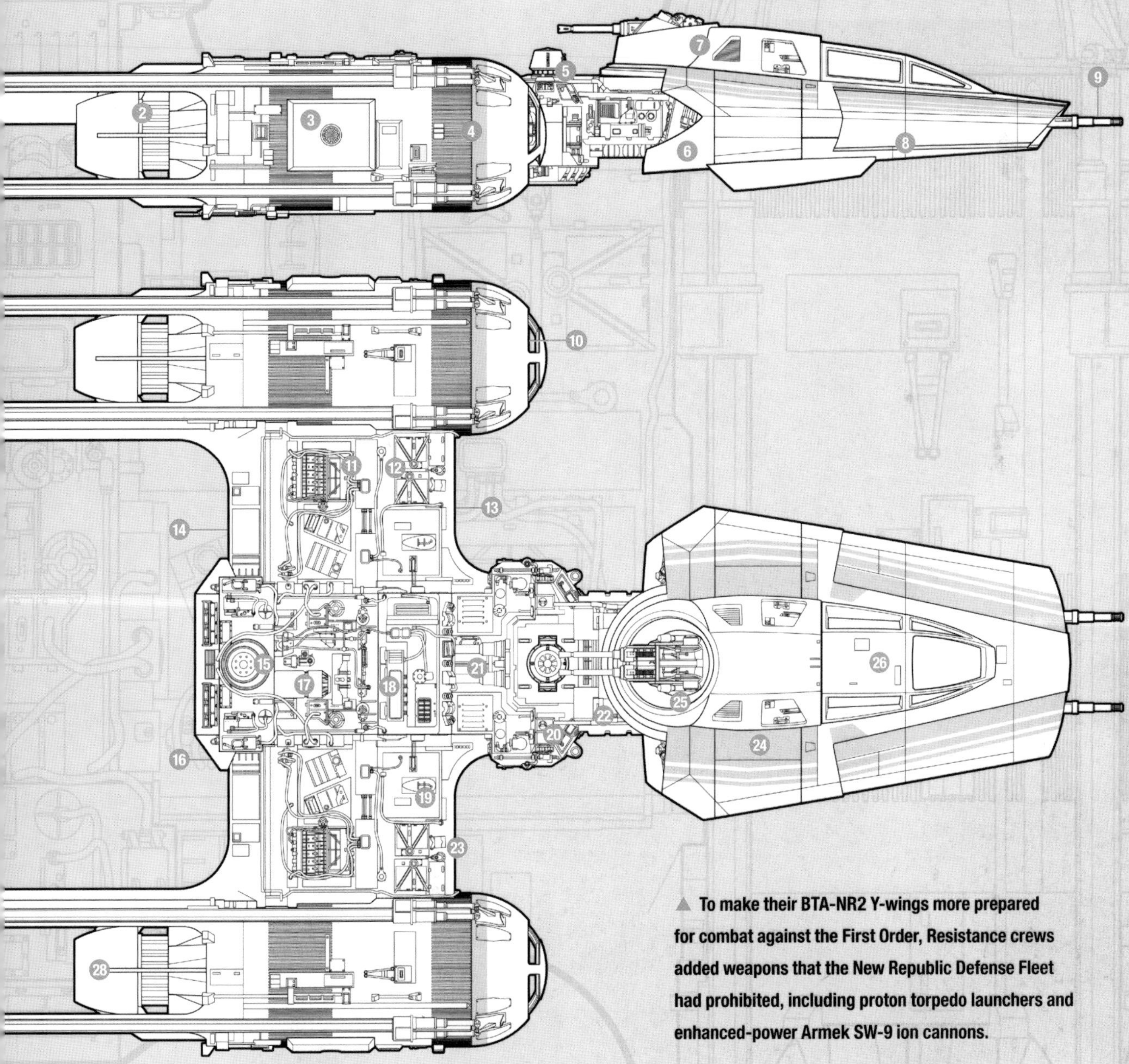

▲ To make their BTA-NR2 Y-wings more prepared for combat against the First Order, Resistance crews added weapons that the New Republic Defense Fleet had prohibited, including proton torpedo launchers and enhanced-power Armek SW-9 ion cannons.

PILOTS, TRAINING, AND GEAR

Excerpt from Admiral Ackbar's *The Pilot and the Rebellion*, required viewing during Alliance recruitment sessions.

The Rebel pilot is the first, and often the last, line of defense between the Empire and the "home fires." Imperial fleets are numerous and relentless. The Imperials must, therefore, learn that we are willing to die for our freedom. But, more importantly, they must learn that they too will die for our freedom.

We cannot offer the amount of training flight-time that you would receive at an Imperial Academy. To a certain extent, we also cannot match their available equipment and resources.

But make no mistake, our pilots are the best in the galaxy. That is a fact. We can train you better than the most top-flight professor at the Academy because our instructors are all combat-trained veterans themselves. The training you receive will not be as extensive as the training a pilot receives at an Imperial Academy, but it will be far more intensive. The typical Academy graduate may never see combat, but every one of you will. Repeatedly. Our aim is not to make sure that you are capable of surviving combat with a trained TIE pilot, but to make sure you are capable of defeating a trained TIE pilot.

In addition, ship for ship, our equipment is better than theirs. Our starfighters are sturdier and equipped with energy shields. Some of our fighters are faster than TIE fighters. Others have heavier artillery and firepower. The Empire, because of its unwieldy size and corrupt bureaucracy, relies on a single model of starfighter to fulfill nearly all its needs. Their single-mindedness is their weakness. We will exploit that weakness with our strength, which is versatility.

Always remember, for every three of their ships destroyed, one of ours is an even trade. Yet we cannot afford to match loss for loss. Nor can we afford attrition. We must win outright.

◀ At the Rebel Alliance's Massassi outpost on Yavin 4, transport speeders carry the rebel pilots of Red, Blue, Green, and Gold Squadron from their ready rooms to their waiting starfighters.

STARFIGHTER BASES AND HANGARS

During the Imperial era, the Rebel Alliance established secret bases, temporary outposts, and supply caches in various sectors throughout the galaxy. In their effort to prevent enemies from finding such locations, rebel field agents and scouts sought out worlds in remote and sometimes uncharted territories, far from enemy patrols and standard hyperspace trade routes. Their bases typically housed numerous personnel and infantry units, starfighters, command and communications centers, and equipment and materials for fabricating weapons. Local supplies and terrain often dictated sites, floor plans, and construction techniques for base's hangars.

Decades after the Rebel Alliance defeated the Empire at the Battle of Jakku, and in defiance of the peace treaty signed by representatives of the New Republic and the Galactic Empire, a secret organization of Imperial hard-liners, the First Order, emerged from the Unknown Regions. The rebel hero Leia Organa founded the Resistance, a small, private military group, to monitor the actions of the First Order, but the First Order's warships and armies soon overwhelmed the Resistance, forcing Organa and her allies to flee their base on D'Qar.

▲ **On the moon Yavin 4, rebel engineers transformed an ancient Massassi temple into an outpost that served as the headquarters for the Alliance to Restore the Republic. The outpost included an extensive landing pad and vast hangar for rebel starfighters.**

▲ Forced to abandon their Massassi outpost, the rebels relocated to the ice planet Hoth, where they carved out a glacier, created a network of tunnels, and expanded natural caverns to create Echo Base, which included hangars for rebel starfighters and airspeeders.

▲ The Mon Calamari MC80 Star Cruiser *Home One* served as the Rebel Alliance's mobile headquarters before the Battle of Endor. One of *Home One*'s large hangar bays accommodated a modified Corellian YT-1300 freighter and a stolen Imperial *Lambda*-class shuttle in addition to X-wing, Y-wing, and A-wing starfighters.

▲ The Resistance base on D'Qar maintained two primary X-wing squadrons, code-named Red and Blue. Blue Squadron was the primary line of defense for the base, with Red Squadron flying as support.

STARFIGHTER MAINTENANCE AND TECHNICAL SUPPORT

Rebel and later Resistance mechanics, technicians, and related starfighter ground crews were among the unsung heroes of the support services that assisted the Alliance Starfighter Command and the Resistance Starfighter Corps. The Rebel Alliance Special Forces, or SpecForces, also included mechanics and other specialists to maintain and repair starships. Some members of SpecForces also served with the Procurement and Supply divisions, which were in charge of liberating ordnance, fuel, and other material from Imperial-occupied worlds. Without such extensive support services, neither the Alliance nor the Resistance would have been able to maintain operations.

The Alliance and Resistance also relied on countless droids to assist with the repair and maintenance of starfighters. Ubiquitous astromech droids not only served as astrogation computers and technical support on Y-wing and X-wing starfighters, but also worked alongside industrial maintenance droids to run diagnostics, make repairs, and install upgrades for starfighters with or without astromech sockets.

▼ R-series astromech droids represented the majority of the droid labor pool at the Massassi outpost. With their various built-in and extendable tools, astromechs are equipped to make efficient repairs and fine-tune technological systems and components on starfighters.

▼ Rebel technicians hoisted Industrial Automaton R-series astromech droids and manually loaded them into the astromech sockets on T-65B X-wing and BTL-A4 Y-wing starfighters.

▶ At Echo Base on Hoth, rebel mechanics worked grueling shifts with numerous droids to ensure starfighters and modified airspeeders would be ready for combat or evacuation, and remain operational in sub-freezing temperatures.

▼ Stationed aboard General Leia Organa's flagship, the MC85 Star Cruiser *Raddus*, Resistance starfighter hangar crews and droids make repairs and run diagnotics to make sure every available starfighter is ready for battle.

FLIGHT SUIT
REBEL PILOT

Some Rebel Alliance starfighter pilots learned their skills at Imperial Academies, and either defected to the Alliance or escaped being drafted into the Imperial Starfleet. Other rebel pilots had experience as commercial fliers, helming passenger ships or cargo cruisers across space. And still others were civilian hobbyists or agrarian pilots, who developed their passion for flight in suborbital spacecraft over backwater planets, far from the Core Worlds. Many rebel pilots had a taste for high-speed thrills. All were unified by their desire to end Imperial rule and restore the democratic ideals of the Galactic Republic.

Colors for rebel pilot flight suits varied but most X-wing and Y-wing pilots wore orange flight suits. The flight suits were pressurized and equipped with a life support unit, and had pockets for storing compact tools and emergency gear. Because rebel starfighters had fully pressurized cockpits, standard-issue rebel pilot helmets had transparent visors but otherwise left the face exposed, allowing pilots to breathe freely. Personalized iconography on the helmets occasionally identified a pilot's unit origin, homeworld, or beliefs. Insulated gloves and boots and a lightweight armored flak vest provided additional protection for the pilot.

REBEL PILOT FLIGHT SUIT

1. Insulated helmet
2. Rebel Alliance Symbol
3. Polarized plastex visor
4. Hearing shield
5. Pressurized g-suit
6. Inflatable flak vest
7. Data cylinders
8. Novaldex life support unit
9. Control conduit/life support umbilical
10. Flight belt
11. Document datapad
12. Thermal gloves
13. Guidenhauser ejection harness
14. Stow pockets
15. Knee pocket
16. Leg belt with signal flares and emergency transmitter
17. Insulated boots
18. Positive grip soles

FLIGHT SUIT
RESISTANCE PILOT

Before the First Order's leaders revealed their intensions to crush the New Republic, the founders of the Resistance were already recruiting pilots from planetary defense forces on worlds that had suffered the most under the Empire's oppression. Although many Resistance pilots were born after the fall of the Empire, all grew up hearing tales of Imperial atrocities, and are determined to stop the First Order. Loyal and dedicated to their squadrons, the pilots are eager to honor the ideals of the former Rebel Alliance. In tribute to those who served in the Alliance, many Resistance pilots have adopted the Alliance symbol to adorn their helmets and flight suits.

Resistance X-wing pilots wear "interstellar orange" flight suits equipped with a FreiTek life support unit that is more durable than the Alliance version, easier to operate and repair, and also more adaptable for non-human pilots. Instead of a standard flak vest made of fabric reinforced with woven metal, Resistance pilots wear vests that are both protective and inflatable. Most Resistance pilot helmets have upgraded visors for better visibility, externally-mounted comlinks, and are designed to be worn without a chinstrap.

RESISTANCE PILOT FLIGHT SUIT

1. **Insulated helmet**
2. **Resistance adopted Alliance symbol**
3. **Polarized plastex visor**
4. **Hearing shield**
5. **Pressurized g-suit**
6. **Inflatable flak vest**
7. **Glie-44 blaster pistol**
8. **FreiTek life support unit**
9. **Control conduit/life support umbilical**
10. **Flight belt**
11. **Datapad document pouch**
12. **Reinforced thermal gloves**
13. **Guidenhauser ejection harness**
14. **Stow pockets**
15. **Knee pocket**
16. **Leg belt with signal flares and emergency transmitter**
17. **Insulated boots**
18. **Positive grip soles**

SIZE COMPARISON CHART

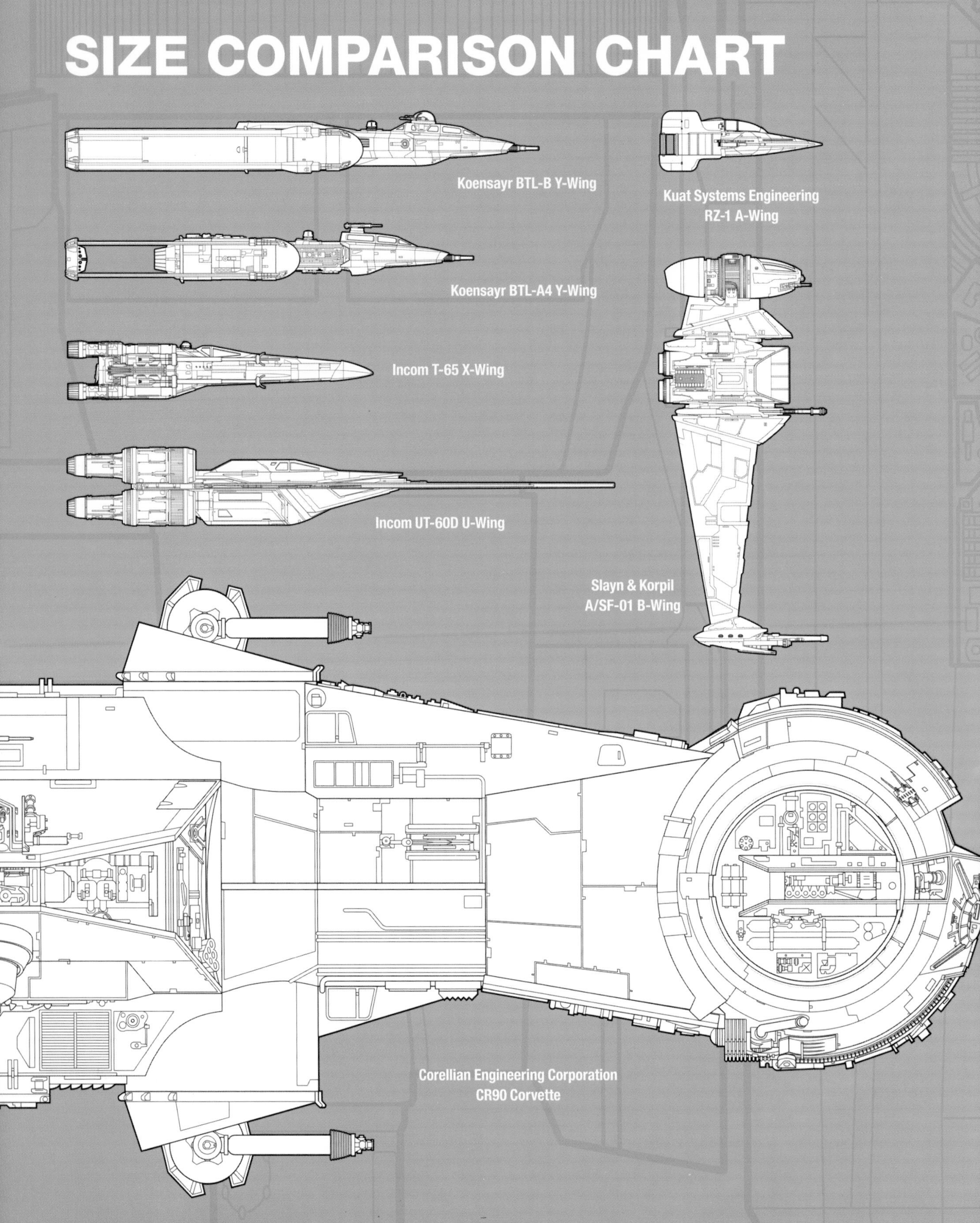

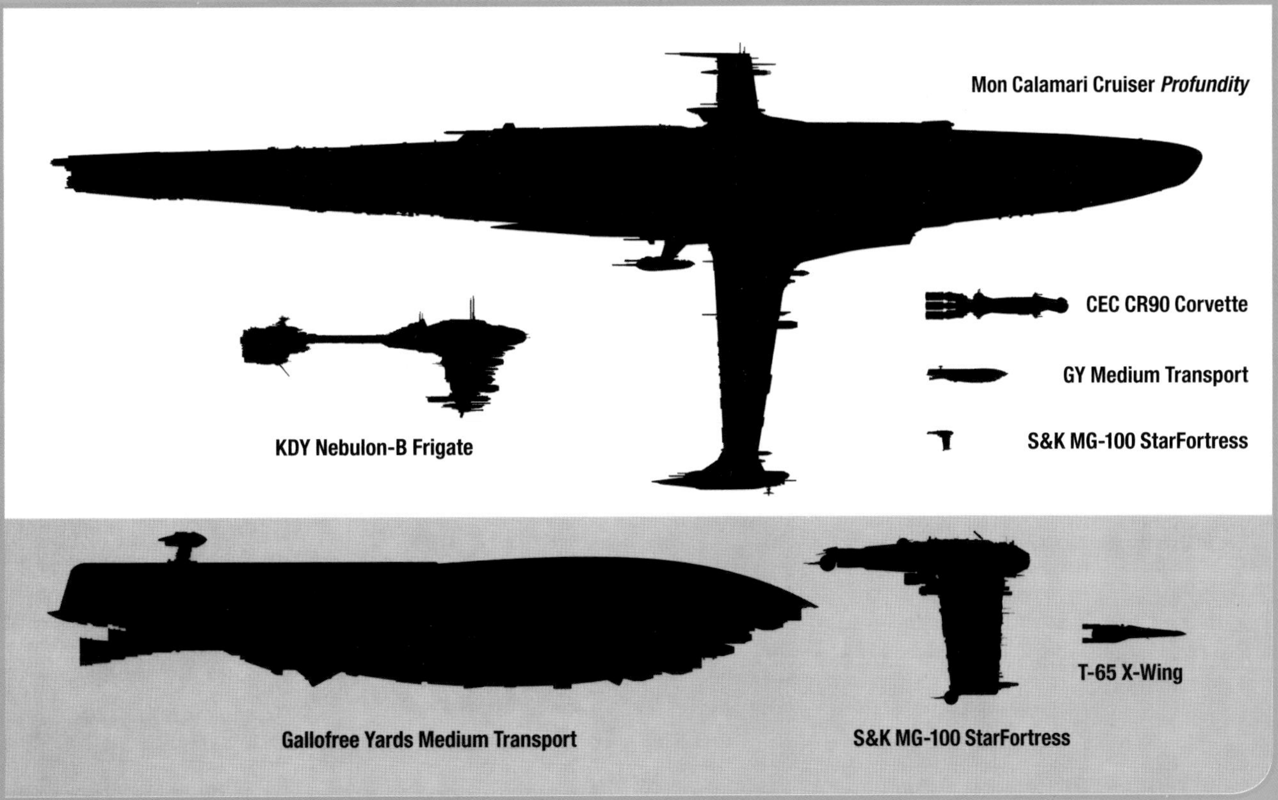

Mon Calamari Cruiser *Profundity*

CEC CR90 Corvette

GY Medium Transport

S&K MG-100 StarFortress

KDY Nebulon-B Frigate

T-65 X-Wing

Gallofree Yards Medium Transport

S&K MG-100 StarFortress

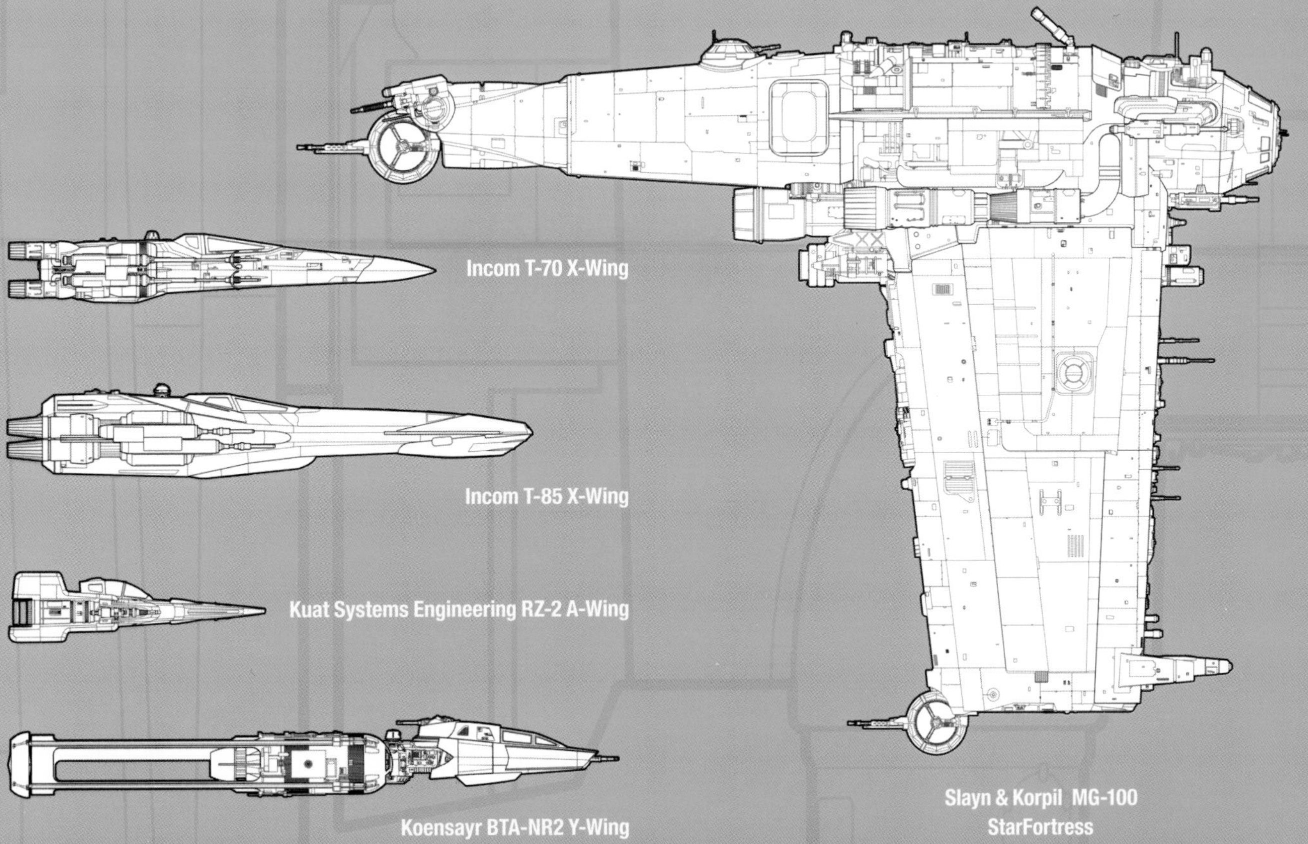

Incom T-70 X-Wing

Incom T-85 X-Wing

Kuat Systems Engineering RZ-2 A-Wing

Koensayr BTA-NR2 Y-Wing

Slayn & Korpil MG-100
StarFortress

ACKNOWLEDGMENTS

The author and artists of the *Rebel Starfighters Owners' Workshop Manual* utilized information about starfighters from many previously published *Star Wars* books, and are indebted to the following writers and artists: Jean-François Boivin, Richard Chasemore, Stephen Crane, Jason Fry, Barbara L. Gibson, Douglas Kaufman, Hans Jenssen, Shane Johnson, Michael Kogge, Paul Murphy, Timothy S. O'Brien, Kemp Remillard, David West Reynolds, Bill Slavicsek, Bill Smith, Curtis Smith, Landry Q. Walker, and Daniel Wallace. We also gratefully acknowledge George Lucas, John Barry, Colin Cantwell, Joe Johnston, Ralph McQuarrie, Lorne Peterson, Paul Huston, and Norman Reynolds and their colleagues for their significant contributions to Rebel starfighters in the *Star Wars* movies.

Special thanks to the following people for their help with reference for this project: Kevin Necessary for his assistance with drawing ship blueprints; Jason Eaton and Joshua Maruska for the use of their digital model greeblies; Sonny Nguyen of Disney Imagineering for his graphic design inspiration; Hez Chorba, Stacey Zimmerman, Tim Mapp, and Michael Mueller of Lucasfilm and ILM for providing 3D game assets; and our friends at Lucasfilm: Troy Alders, Leland Chee, Michael Dailey, Pablo Hidalgo, Samantha Holland, Orion Kellogg, Beatrice Kilat, Nicole LaCoursiere, Matt Martin, Bryce Pinkos, Erik Sanchez, Kesley Sharpe, Michael Siglain, Robert Simpson, and Sarah Williams.

▼ The X-wing starfighter in Ralph McQuarrie's concept painting for *Star Wars* (1977) inspired the design of the next-generation X-wings introduced in *The Force Awakens* (2015).